All Cats Go to Heaven

by

Valda V. Upenieks

Illustrations by Kalpart

Editor: Ausma S. Lidacis

Strategic Book Publishing and Rights Co.

Book Design/Layout, Illustrations and Book Cover design by Kalpart. Visit www.kalpart.com

Strategic Book Publishing and Rights Co.
12620 FM 1960, Suite A4-507
Houston, TX 77065
www.sbpra.com

For information about special discounts for bulk purchases,
please contact Strategic Book Publishing and Rights Co. Special Sales,
at bookorder@sbpra.net.

ISBN: 978-1-63135-645-2

Dedicated to Muris

Muris, at twenty years old, traveled to Cat Heaven during the writing of this story. He was an amazing alpha cat who lived life to his fullest and experienced many places on Earth.

Muris was dominant and very present in each moment. He made all surroundings his territory.

During the last few years of his life, Muris changed. He mellowed and became a very lovable cat. This may have been due to his old age—though I believe an angel cat changed him.

Table of Contents

Part One—Cat Heaven

1. Cat Heaven

My name is Minka. I'm a new angel cat up here in Cat Heaven. I left Earth several months ago. You can find me high above the chimney tops, beyond where the birds fly and with the Earth clouds far behind me.

I'm not really sure how I ended up in Cat Heaven after living only one life on Earth. My best friend on Earth, Muris, told me that cats are allowed nine lives. Yet somehow I ended up in Cat Heaven after leaving Earth for the first time. Maybe my nine lives were jumbled up into one really long life. After all, I did live twice as long as most Earth cats, as I was seventeen years old when I left Earth. It may have been because I was really kind during my time on Earth. I did teach many of my cat friends good lessons. Those deeds may have been enough to get me through the Doors of Cat Heaven after my first life.

As I sit on my angel cloud and look around Cat Heaven, I realize it's actually not much different from Earth. Everything is peaceful, bright, and beautiful. There are many other angel cats

9

here just like me, resting or sleeping on their angel clouds. The air is always fresh and has the scent of summer days. A warm breeze sways the heavenly trees back and forth. The birds chirp all sorts of angel melodies from their nests in the trees. I no longer try to catch the birds, but rather just listen to their tunes. The flowers are always in full bloom, with an abundance of fragrances. The angel bees and butterflies fly around in the flowerbeds and play with one another. The grass around my angel cloud is tall, soft, and lavishly green. The heavenly grasshoppers jump here and there and sing their own festive tunes. We all get along up here.

When I first arrived in Cat Heaven, my angel buddy, Chloe, greeted me. "Hello, Minka, welcome to Cat Heaven," her warm purring voice said as I landed on my new angel cloud. "You are even more beautiful than you were on Earth. Your white and black fur is soft and flawless, your tail still has that glowing speck of white fur at its tip, and your eyes are ever so hazel green."

I felt as though I saw my own reflection in Chloe. She was identical to me—peaceful-looking and distinguished. She had almost the same soft markings that I did. Her fur was angel white and black, yet she had a few more brown markings around her back, tail, and face. Her left ear was covered with black fur and her right ear was white, just like mine. Chloe even had the same dark patch covering her left eye, except that my patch was black and hers was brown.

Chloe told me that she would be with me every day as my angel buddy during this first phase of Cat Heaven before I ascend to Higher Cat Heaven.

She explained the rules of the first phase of Cat Heaven. I was not to travel far from my angel cloud, though I could climb the trees and eat the grass surrounding my angel cloud.

Chloe also had no hesitation explaining her strict regimen for

me in Cat Heaven (which was not all that strict). I would slowly wake up each morning on my angel cloud, and then yawn and stretch while my tail twitched back and forth. Chloe would greet me with a wonderful breakfast served on my angel cloud (back on Earth, Muris and I had to find our way to our cat dish when breakfast was being served).

After breakfast would come bath time. Chloe would lather me with a lot of oils and soap. I wasn't certain I would like having a bath each day, because on Earth I was able to keep myself clean. Chloe insisted that I keep my long white and black fur shining. The rest of the day was to be spent on my angel cloud, marking my new territory with my nose, kneading my cloud, climbing a tree to hear the birds chirping their songs, or sleeping—but I would always be awakened by Chloe for lunch and dinner.

Twice a week Chloe would fly with me over to the Heavenly Cat Auditorium, where the angel cats would get to know and play with one another. Sometimes there would be updates about new changes in Cat Heaven, but for the most part it would be a social event. I ended up sticking to myself and watching the angel cats mingling with each other.

***

One morning after breakfast, as I was getting ready for my bath, Chloe told me that during this phase of Cat Heaven I could have any Earthly wish fulfilled. According to Chloe, the wish was to be something I felt was left undone on Earth. It was a way of purging the past before ascending properly into Cat Heaven.

I thought hard. I was very much loved on Earth by my owner, Valerie, and was able to do what I wanted to do. My needs were met. Only one wish popped into my head: the desire to fly back to Earth in order to see my cat friends, whom I missed.

"Oh, Minka," Chloe cried, "please ask me for another wish! I can't allow you to go back to Earth just to be with your friends." My angel buddy whisked her tail back and forth. "Your wish must have a *purpose*. There must be some other Earthly need—something you wish you had one more chance to complete. Look at all the other angel cats—they are being granted their wishes and are very happy."

I looked around and noticed a large number of cats munching on heavenly treats while others chased birds all around their angel clouds. Various angel cats were pouncing on mice that were burrowing their clouds. Many cats were being pampered, given a bath once a day, sometimes even twice.

"Minka, the cats here in Cat Heaven are granted a wish that was not fulfilled while on Earth," explained Chloe. "Some of the angel cats were always hungry, and that's why they asked for heavenly treats all day long. Certainly we do not over-feed the angel cats in Cat Heaven, but they are given all the food they desire until their tummies are content. Other angel cats lacked affection on Earth, so they are pampered with extra baths and heavenly compassion. Many angel cats could not fulfill their instinct to hunt prey on Earth, so we provide them with birds and mice to chase. Of course, they never catch them, but we give them the chance to try!"

I was puzzled. None of those needs had gone unmet on Earth.

"There must be *some* wish that wasn't fulfilled for you," meowed Chloe.

I thought for a long while. My tail flicked back and forth and I licked my front paws. I was treated really well on Earth. I was given a lot of food, love, warmth, and affection by Valerie. We even had a few other animals join our household: a cat named Sofia and a dog named Lana. But that did not bother Muris and me, as we were always happy to be together. I lived in different places, but always with my best friend, Muris. We even had the chance to live in California, where I basked in the hot sun by the pool every day. That was probably why I lived as long as I did.

Then a new thought occurred to me.

"I want to go down to Earth to protect my friends from any harm or danger," I stated.

"Well, that's better than just stopping by for a visit—now there is a purpose to your wish," Chloe said as she peered into my eyes. "But it may not be possible. A wish such as yours has never been granted to an angel cat. It would take a lot of doing."

"But you will think about it?"

"Yes, I will," Chloe said, though she sounded hesitant. "In the meantime, is there a simpler task you can think about completing instead?"

"No. I can't think of another wish," I told Chloe, giving her a wink as I purred.

Chloe turned and flew away from me, and I gazed down at my angel cloud. I pushed my head deeper into the cloud. I looked through the cloud dust until finally I saw a vision of Earth!

I was so excited that I stood straight up on my angel cloud. I peered again, farther down, and found I could see far, far below me. My tail began to twitch wildly back and forth.

This was amazing! I was able to see right where I used to live. I even saw Muris, running to his cat dish for his morning meal. *Hmm*, I thought to myself, *maybe this is the beginning of my Earthly wish . . .*

2. Willie

New angel cats arrive in Cat Heaven the same way I did: once a cat leaves Earth, the angel cat ascends through the clouds. The angel cat travels for miles and miles and finally enters the fresh, clean ozone layer of the Heavenly World. There, the angel cat is met by a guide helper.

Guide helpers are cats who have nearly completed the first phase of Cat Heaven. Their Earthly wish has been granted, but since they weren't the friendliest cats while on Earth, they must work harder to dismiss their bad deeds before entering Higher Cat Heaven. As helpers, their intentions must be pure—otherwise they will remain in the first phase of Cat Heaven forever. Their responsibilities consist of greeting new cats as they arrive in Cat Heaven as well as patrolling the area to make sure the angel cats stay on or very near to their angel clouds.

All the guide helpers have small, pure-white wings honoring their position in Cat Heaven. Their wings make a loud *rat-ta-ta* flapping sound. The guide helpers must flap their wings to stay afloat. They can only fly at a certain height and in one direction at a time.

The air is very light when a new angel cat reaches the ozone layer of Cat Heaven. The guide helper helps the angel cat stay afloat by holding on to his or her neck and flying up to the Doors of Cat Heaven.

Once the doors open, the new angel cat is free to trot into Cat Heaven while the guide helper flies overhead. Kittens and young cats who have left Earth usually run wild when they enter the Doors of Cat Heaven, enjoying the feel of pure, light air. The older and more mature cats look around, sniff their new surroundings, and mark the new territory with their scent glands. Then they put one paw in front of the other and step inside Cat Heaven before meeting their angel buddy for the first time.

Angel buddies are angel cats who have been in Cat Heaven for a period of time. They served a social guidance role on Earth and decided to continue with these duties in Cat Heaven. The process of becoming a new angel buddy is very rigorous. They are tested, interviewed, and trained by current angel buddies. This allows the new angel buddy to learn how to help angel cats fulfill their Earthly wishes. If they pass their training, new angel buddies must vow under oath to uphold the sacred rules of Cat Heaven. The angel buddies are committed to staying in the first phase of Cat Heaven to fulfill their sacred duties before ascending to Higher Cat Heaven.

Angel buddies have big, beautiful white wings outlined in gold. Their wings make a softly fluttering, lulling sound. They don't have to flap their wings to stay afloat; rather, their wings can keep them suspended in air and let them make twirls, swirls, and dives.

An angel buddy is chosen for each new angel cat entering Cat

Heaven based on matching qualities such as temperament, coloring, age, and get-along-ability. Once a new angel cat is greeted by an angel buddy, he or she is guided to an angel cloud, bathed, fed, and then left to rest after the long journey.

The first day after a new angel cat has arrived in Cat Heaven is the most difficult time for an angel buddy. He or she must be very patient. The angel buddy needs to introduce him or herself, explain what Cat Heaven is all about, and start the ritual of helping a cat decide on an Earthly wish that needs to be fulfilled.

New angel cats or kittens arrive on a daily basis at the Doors of Cat Heaven. Sometimes many cats enter at the same time, while at other times a few trickle in here or there. If it is a bad traffic day, just like on Earth, each angel cat tries to mark his or her territory, and a bit of hissing and scratching takes place. The guide helpers have to make order out of the chaos.

***

My angel cloud is placed at the perfect spot. I have an ideal view of the angel cats entering the Doors of Cat Heaven. I like to watch them entering so I can see all the different kinds of cats who have lived on Earth.

One morning, well before breakfast, I was watching the Doors of Cat Heaven open. A young black-and-white cat ran quickly through the doors. He was very excited and energetic. There was a wild yet adorable karma about him. Black fur covered his back and face, while soft white baby fur covered his tummy and all four paws.

The young cat peered around, paused, and then looked directly at me. He came running over and pounced on my angel cloud.

I recognized him immediately. "Willie!"

"Minka, I am so happy to see you!" he responded as his tail

twitched about.

"What are you doing here? There must be some sort of mistake—you are too young to be in Cat Heaven," I said. "I would have expected one of the older cats in our neighborhood to be marching through the Doors of Cat Heaven before you!"

"No, it's not a mistake. I got stuck outside in the cold weather for a whole day and night. It was raining and I got real hungry and cold. I might have eaten something that wasn't good for me, or maybe it was the dampness. Anyway, when I went back inside the next morning, I couldn't stop shivering and sneezing," Willie explained. "Casper . . ."

"Oh, yes, the two of you were inseparable!" I interrupted. "I remember the times Muris and I would jump on top of the fence and peer into your house and see you playing or sleeping together. The two of you were stuck together like glue!"

"Casper would have protected me, but it was my fault I got stuck outside. He tried to get out too, but Anna accidentally shut the front door behind me," Willie said.

"I remember your owner—she was just as sweet as ours! Anna always fussed over the two of you!" I exclaimed.

"If Casper had been with me, things would have gone a lot better. He has a strong sense of the outdoors and street smarts about him," Willie went on.

"That's a shame," I sighed, and nudged Willie's face.

"I was sick for about one week. Anna was so worried that she even brought me to the doctor. She did everything to help me get better. Nothing helped, not even the medicine—and now here I am," Willie meowed softly.

"My precious Willie, I am so saddened that you had to leave Earth on such short notice and aren't able to spend any more time with Casper," I stated as tears filled my eyes.

"I do miss Casper, but I am really glad you are here with me," he said, and purred.

"I will make Cat Heaven feel like home to you, even though I have not been here much longer than you. In fact, I'll ask Chloe if I can share my angel cloud with you. And I'll find out what happened to your other eight lives."

"That would be nice," Willie said, and then added, "Who is Chloe? What eight lives?"

Just then, Chloe appeared with Oscar, a young cat who looked exactly like Willie—black fur on his back and head, white fur accenting his tummy and paws.

"Willie, you ran through the Doors of Cat Heaven so quickly that I lost track of you," Oscar exclaimed. "And now here you are with Minka!"

Willie stared at Oscar.

"I am your angel buddy," Oscar informed him. "I will spend time with you every day."

"That sounds like fun," exclaimed Willie, as he leaped around on my angel cloud.

I looked at Willie and then Oscar. They had exactly the same movements. I reckoned they did a pretty good job in Cat Heaven in finding the perfect angel buddy for each of us. Oscar had the same mannerisms and youthfulness as Willie, including his lack of concentration!

"I can understand why I may have not been granted my other eight lives," I told Chloe, "but what about Willie?"

"I am not sure—I really don't know," she answered.

Oscar chimed in. "Maybe Willie will be a special angel cat here in Cat Heaven."

Chloe turned and hissed, "Don't make up an answer just for the sake of having one. We need to speak the truth in Cat Heaven."

"Well, I might be speaking the truth," Oscar shot back. "I have an awfully good feeling about Willie!"

"Can the two of us share an angel cloud?" I asked.

"Definitely not. No sharing clouds. Willie needs his own angel cloud in order to be cleaned and fed, and so he can be with Oscar. But I will arrange for Willie's angel cloud to be next to yours," Chloe announced.

And there it was. Our angel clouds were placed next to one another's, and we were happy!

3. An Earthly Wish

When Willie and I were not attended to by our angel buddies, we spent time with each other, which made Chloe a bit concerned. She felt this was not allowing us to expand our horizons and make friends with the other angel cats in Cat Heaven. On the other hand, perhaps Willie and I would discuss our Earthly wishes with each other. Chloe hoped that Willie would request a simple Earthly wish and inspire me to tone down my desire to visit Earth again. Oscar, on the other hand, was grateful for my guidance with Willie since he was new in his role and wasn't quite sure what to do with him.

Early one morning, after Willie and I had been fed and bathed, I asked Willie over to my angel cloud. "Look below—no, Willie, put your head way down into my cloud."

"Wow," he exclaimed, "I can see Earth!" Willie peered deeper down through the cloud. "I can see far, far below me. I can even see where I used to live!"

"Keep looking," I told him.

"Oh, my gosh! I can see Casper grooming himself after his morning meal!" Willie meowed excitedly.

"Pretty cool," I agreed.

"You bet! I would be very happy to just sit here all day on your angel cloud and watch over Casper!" exclaimed Willie as he kneaded my cloud and twitched his tail in excitement.

"Willie, has Oscar asked you about fulfilling an Earthly wish?" I asked as I paced back and forth on my cloud.

"Mmm, yeah, kind of," Willie said as he gazed at Casper far, far below.

"Have you told him what you want that wish to be?" I asked, lying next to Willie.

"Sort of, but it's not really a wish I want to do. I can't figure out what I really need to do. Every time I think of something, Oscar just nods and tells me he will get back to me about whether the wish can be fulfilled," Willie replied.

"What about asking Oscar if you can fly back to Earth with me to protect Casper and our other friends?" I asked as I groomed the fur on his chest.

"That would be awesome! But how would that work? How could we get back down to Earth?"

"With wings," I answered, and went on with my grooming.

Willie paused, thought for a moment, and imagined himself with big, huge wings. He kneaded my angel cloud and then looked at me and grinned.

"The next time Oscar asks about your Earthly wish, tell him you want to fly back down to Earth with me. See what he says," I remarked as my tail twitched back and forth.

"I sure will," Willie promised.

As we had planned, the next morning while Oscar was carefully bathing Willie, he remarked, "I know what I want my Earthly wish to be."

"Great, let's hear it!" meowed Oscar.

"I want to fly back to Earth with Minka to protect our friends from danger," Willie said matter-of-factly.

Oscar immediately stopped scrubbing Willie behind the ears. He gazed at him and then looked nervously over his shoulders and back again. "Hmm, I'm not at all certain that we can make that kind of wish happen in Cat Heaven."

"Why not?" Willie immediately prompted. "Ask Chloe. I'm sure she will agree."

"Well, all right," Oscar said. He quickly gathered up the bathing things and flew over to see Chloe, who was hovering above our clouds.

As soon as Oscar had left, Willie pounced over onto my angel cloud. He told me about his conversation with Oscar. I nudged his head and purred. The two of us positioned ourselves next to each other and looked up at Chloe and Oscar, who were flying in circles and absorbed in a deep conversation.

The discussion went on for a while between the two. Every once in a while, Chloe would look down at us and then back at Oscar. I could tell she was deep in thought.

Finally Chloe and Oscar flew down to my angel cloud. Chloe took her place beside me, while Oscar nervously flapped his wings and flew above Willie.

"Well, this is some Earthly wish that the two of you have come up with," Chloe began as she leaped to the other side of my cloud. "I'm not certain it can be granted, because no other angel cat has ever asked to fly back down to Earth before."

Willie and I sat still and waited.

"My first inclination was to say absolutely not," Chloe went on. "Yet my gut keeps nudging me. This wish may lead to something good, something more than I can understand right now. After all, your wish is about helping your cat friends on Earth—and as Oscar and I are angel buddies, we must support good deeds."

Willie excitedly paced around my angel cloud. I kept still so I could hear what Chloe had to say.

"If your intentions are pure, and your Earthly wish is not just a way to play with your cat friends on Earth again, I will speak with the Angel Leaders to see if there is a way we can grant it," Chloe meowed, leaping back to my side of the cloud.

"Our intentions are very real. Who are these Angel Leaders you must speak with?" I asked.

"The Angel Leaders are our bosses. They oversee all of Cat Heaven—the first phase, which you are in, as well as Higher Cat Heaven, which is the only place where true cat purity exists. There are seven Angel Leaders—four males and three females. One Angel Leader position is vacant. The Angel Leaders can't find a perfect angel cat to fill the vacant role," Chloe explained.

"Wow," Willie remarked, his tail switching back and forth excitedly.

"The Angel Leaders live in that big Angel Castle to the north, toward the path to Higher Cat Heaven," Chloe continued. "They are very powerful and wise. The Angel Leaders have a passionate ability to love all angel cats as well as a wish to bring peace, hope, and change to Cat Heaven. They have a synergistic quality, a talent in bringing out the moral spirits of all angel cats for the goodness of Higher Cat Heaven."

"My gosh!" Willie sounded totally amazed. "I wouldn't know what to say or do if I ever met one of the Angel Leaders."

"Don't worry, Willie," Oscar said kindly. "Angel cats never meet the Angel Leaders during the first part of Cat Heaven. Only angel buddies are allowed to enter the Angel Castle."

I said nothing. I had a strange feeling about the Angel Leaders. Somehow I understood their purpose and felt connected to them. But it wasn't something I could explain to Willie, or even to Chloe.

"When you complete your Earthly wishes and are allowed to move into Higher Cat Heaven, you will fly over the Angel Castle," Chloe told us.

"So will you go and speak with the Angel Leaders?" I meowed.

"Yes, Oscar and I both will. But that does not mean that your Earthly wish will be granted," Chloe reminded us. "By the way, how do you two plan to travel down to Earth? This may be a very important detail to tell our bosses."

"With wings! Big, beautiful, feathered wings," I explained.

"I see," Chloe said in a measured voice, while Oscar nervously flapped his own wings.

They flew off, promising to get back to us. We watched them fly high above us and then turn north in the direction of the Angel Castle.

4. The Rules

Willie and I waited patiently on my cloud for Chloe and Oscar to return. We waited and waited. Night fell.

"I'm not certain Chloe and Oscar will return tonight," I told Willie as I yawned and began to knead my angel cloud sleepily.

"Do you think that they have forgotten about our Earthly wish?" he asked.

"Actually, I think it may be a good sign," I meowed. "If the Angel Leaders felt that our Earthly wish wasn't a good idea, Chloe and Oscar would have returned right away."

Willie nodded. I slowly started to push him in the direction of his angel cloud.

"They are probably having a long discussion to see if they can work out all the details," I said and yawned again.

"What details? It's simple—we get our wings and we fly to Earth," Willie stated matter-of-factly.

I chuckled at Willie's innocent ease in capturing the simple facts of our angel existence.

"Let's get some rest," I meowed. "Go on, it's time for bed." I pushed Willie one more time in the direction of his angel cloud.

"Be sure to wake me early in the morning. I don't want to miss a thing!" Willie exclaimed as he pounced over to his own cloud. He snuggled into a small ball and instantly fell asleep.

As soon as Willie left my angel cloud, I, too, fell fast asleep.

Early the next morning, I nudged Willie awake. "Willie, wake up," I purred as I licked his forehead. "Come over to my angel cloud so we can wait for Chloe and Oscar to arrive."

After a long time, I could see Chloe and Oscar on the far horizon, flying directly toward our angel clouds. They settled down in front of us.

Chloe looked at Willie and then at me. "We have some good news. The Angel Leaders have agreed to fulfill your Earthly wish."

Willie began to jump around on my angel cloud with pure joy. Even Oscar did a few somersaults.

"Several of the guide helpers will build your wings and teach you how to fly. This will take place during the night when the other angel cats are sleeping. The guide helpers will be sworn to secrecy, since no other angel cats will be allowed to know about your Earthly wish," Chloe stated sternly. "The Angel Leaders felt that if the other angel cats knew, they might feel the two of you have been granted special treatment.

"The guide helpers have their best vision at night," she went on, "so they will be able to work quickly and use the strongest materials for your wings. Once you have mastered flying, you will be required to perform a test flight before you receive the final okay from the Angel Leaders to complete your Earthly wish," Chloe

finished as she paced back and forth on my angel cloud, wings softly fluttering.

Willie and I nodded. We could hardly wait to start flying!

"But . . ." She paused. "You must agree to abide by five sacred rules."

"And those are?" Impatiently, I switched my tail back and forth.

"The first is that the two of you can select only four cats to protect on Earth. Second, each of these cats must have a real need for your guidance," Chloe explained as she stopped pacing. "The third rule is that you can only visit each cat three times—and for only four hours at a time. If you surpass your time limit during any of these visits, the Earthly cat will not learn anything from the two of you," Chloe announced, leaping near to where Willie was sitting.

"And the fourth rule?" I asked.

"The fourth rule is that if an Earthly cat is truly helped, you must allow them to see or feel some form of the Heavenly vision during your last visit with them," Chloe meowed.

"How can that happen?" I asked.

"You must let them see or feel your presence," stated Chloe.

I wasn't quite sure what Chloe meant by Heavenly vision, and I was sure Willie didn't know either. Finally I decided it was a moot point, since there were so many hurdles to pass before we ever reached a Heavenly vision.

"What's the last rule?" Willie asked shyly.

"Ah, that's the most important rule," Chloe said. She flew over Willie and landed next to Oscar. "At the end of this trial period, if all four cats have been protected and helped, you must ask yourselves why you needed to do what you did for your friends."

"The fourth rule seems tough enough," I complained, "but the fifth rule sounds even more difficult. I'm not really sure what it means."

"If and when the time comes, you will," Chloe assured me. "Now," she went on, "I suggest you two rest for the remainder of the day. The guide helpers will arrive at your angel clouds at midnight to begin building your wings." Chloe and Oscar then fluttered away into the sky.

Willie looked at me in amazement. "Are you sure we can do this?"

"I'm sure we can," I responded.

I wasn't really sure, but I didn't want to put any doubt in Willie's mind. In fact, I wasn't really sure what we were getting ourselves into. This had turned into much more than I'd originally planned. I had no idea there would be sacred rules to follow or that Willie and I could falter before completing our Earthly wish.

Then I remembered that I was in Cat Heaven, and that powerful forces were guiding our destiny on a much larger scale than I had ever felt on Earth. I remembered Chloe's words. I would just have to trust and be patient.

5. Wings

At exactly midnight, Willie and I were awakened by the four cat guide helpers who were assigned to this secret project by the Angel Leaders. The guide helpers were the best of the best and had been sworn to absolute secrecy. Willie and I heard their loud *rat-ta-ta* wings flying above our angel clouds. Each carried a large bag filled with heavenly bird feathers and a sewing kit.

Willie's eyes fluttered open. When he realized that the guide helpers were on his angel cloud to begin building his wings, he leaped in the air and then rushed around on his cloud in total excitement.

"Can we help you guys?" I asked the two guide helpers, who were busy organizing their sewing tools on my angel cloud.

"Not tonight. We just need to get your and Willie's measurements so we can decide how large to make your wings," one of the guide helpers replied as she took her measuring tape from her sewing kit.

Then the guide helpers began to measure my back and all four legs, as well as my ears and paws. "Why do you need all these measurements?" I asked as my tail twitched back and forth. "Shouldn't the length of my back be enough to build my wings?"

"Oh, no," the other guide helper replied. "It is very important that your wings be in perfect balance with the rest of your body. Certainly your back is the most important measurement, followed by your legs. But if your right ear is too large or too small for the size of the right wing, you will not be able to fly in the right direction. Same goes for the left ear. Your paws play a major role in helping you take off and land. If your wings are too small or too large compared to the size of your paws, you might crash when you land. We don't want that to happen! So it's best to let us get all the measurements we need without making a fuss."

I stood by in silence. I decided not to ask too many questions, but just let the guide helpers do what they were sent to do. If they needed my help, they would let me know.

Willie, on the other hand, was so excited that he kept leaping from one end of his angel cloud to the other. The two guide helpers assisting him were having a difficult time getting him to stand still.

"Hey, Willie," I called, "calm down! I'm just as excited as you are. But it's really important that you let the guide helpers get the measurements for your wings so that we can fly down to Earth to help our friends."

"Oh, all right," he grumbled. "I just can't believe it. I'm going to have wings!" he exclaimed, leaping into the air and landing next to one of the guide helpers.

Even though Willie's restlessness put the guide helpers behind schedule, they didn't let their frustration show. Up in Cat Heaven,

cats feel the same emotions they did on Earth, but they only express positive emotions.

After all our measurements were taken, the guide helpers outlined the border of our wings in magical flying wire. Next, they opened large bags filled with feathers and rummaged around until they found just the feathers they were looking for. The guide helpers carefully attached Heavenly golden seagull feathers around the edges of our wings. Seagull feathers have a lot of speed as well as the ability to navigate perfectly. These were the best choice to keep our wings stable and give us the swiftness we needed to take off, turn, and land.

Then the guide helpers placed the outlined wings on our backs and took a few more measurements. They insisted on making sure that we both had the right wing balance and proportion.

Willie seemed totally amazed. "Minka, just look at how big my wings are going to be!"

"I'm sure they will be," I responded with a big meow.

After the guide helpers attached the outlined wings to my back, I, too, was astonished at the size. They were going to be so big that I wasn't sure how I was going to carry them on my back. By the time all the feathers were attached, the wings would be so heavy!

As soon as the guide helpers completed our final measurements, they swiftly gathered up their sewing kits, the bags filled with feathers, and our outlined wings, and flew away into the darkness with a loud *rat-ta-ta* flapping sound.

"I wonder where they are going to keep our wings," Willie said.

"I'm not sure. Maybe in the Angel Castle. The Angel Leaders might need to inspect the wings before we leave," I answered, and then yawned and licked my paws.

"Cool—I'm glad the wings are going to be kept safe at the Angel Castle!"

"I'm not positive about that, but maybe," I responded sleepily. "Come on, I think we should get some rest—it's almost two in the morning, and Oscar and Chloe will be waking us early for breakfast."

Willie was consumed with joy. He tossed and turned and even talked to himself about the size of his wings until he fell fast asleep. I was exhausted, but I, too, felt very excited.

The next morning Chloe and Oscar had trouble waking us up. But once the day began, Willie and I could not keep our excitement contained, especially around the other angel cats. All day long, Willie and I winked at each other and nudged our heads together. Luckily, since cats are independent by nature, the other cats didn't take much notice of us. They were occupied with their own Earthly wishes.

For the next week, the same routine unfolded. The guide helpers appeared at our angel clouds at exactly midnight. Most of the time was spent carefully sewing each heavenly bird feather to our wings. A powerful flying thread was used to stitch them together.

On the eighth visit, the guide helpers completed our wings. With a loud *rat-ta-ta*, they flew to our angel clouds carrying our Heavenly wings.

Willie and I looked at our wings with amazement. "Wow!" exclaimed Willie. "They are absolutely beautiful."

"They even glow," I purred. My wings were eight inches long and a foot wide, and were made of thousands of bird feathers. The two wings were identical. The individual feathers glowed and created a beautiful tapestry of colors. The inner section was covered with yellow bird feathers as bright as the sun's rays, and the middle section had robin feathers as rich as red roses. Bluebird feathers, as serene and deep blue as the ocean, covered the outermost part. The golden seagull feathers that outlined my wings sparkled and gave them a magical and heavenly appearance.

Willie's wings were a bit smaller—seven inches in length and nine inches wide—though they had nearly the same amount of feathers as mine. His had no pattern, but rather a mixture of yellow, red, and blue feathers scattered throughout. Each feather was striking. The seagull feathers that outlined his wings glowed, giving his wings a magical shimmer.

"And now, the final touch," one of the guide helpers announced. Each of the four guide helpers opened a jar filled with golden dust. "This is heavenly catnip, which will provide both of your wings with the magical power they need to fly."

The guide helpers raised their paws and sprinkled the heavenly catnip over our wings. "Tomorrow night we will try your first test flight."

The guide helpers gathered their sewing tools and our big, beautiful wings and flew away into the darkness. The loud *rat-ta-ta* flapping sound of their wings became faint and finally disappeared.

"Tomorrow night I get to fly!" Willie exclaimed. I could still hear him rattling away about flying up in the air as I dozed off into a deep sleep.

6. I Can Fly

The next day, Willie and I tried to keep our excitement about learning to fly to ourselves. We didn't talk much to Chloe and Oscar, even though they knew about our Earthly wish. Instead, we just went about our normal routine and patiently waited for darkness to arrive.

At midnight, the four guide helpers appeared at our angel clouds. They carried our big, beautiful wings with them. The four took their places in front of our clouds and smiled.

Willie and I smiled back. My tail moved swiftly back and forth. "So, how do we get the wings onto our backs?" I asked.

"We thought you would never ask!" one of the guide helpers joked.

"Your angel wings will instantly appear on your back when you chant eight magical words," another guide helper meowed.

I thought he was joking, too. "What are they?" I hesitantly meowed back.

"*Sastik, mastic, kulik, pelik, skeber, veber, milip*, tips," they replied in unison.

"Excuse me?" I asked as my tail lashed back and forth wildly.

"It's okay, Minka," Willie said. "The guide helpers just sneezed."

I was getting annoyed but tried to stay calm. "I know Willie and I are excited to get our Earthly wish started, and we might be asking silly questions, but please tell us how to get the wings on our backs," I meowed.

"By saying *sastik, mastic, kulik, pelik, skeber, veber, milip, tips.*" Once again the guide helpers repeated the strange words in unison.

"They're the eight magical words. Try saying them out loud," one of the guide helpers said as all four moved onto my angel cloud.

"Well, okay." I cleared my throat and recited the words in my head. "*Sastik, mastic, kulik, pelik, skeber, veber, milip, tips!*" I exclaimed. At once my wings magically appeared on my back! I turned my head and saw them sparkling. They felt as light as the feathers they were made from!

"Now you try, Willie," the next guide helper said.

"*Shustik, mushtic*—um . . ."

"No, it's *sastik, mastic, kulik, pelik, skeber, veber, milip, tips,*" all of them repeated in unison as they moved to Willie's cloud.

Willie tried again. "*Pelik, skeber, veber, milip, tips . . .*"

"Almost there," they encouraged.

"You have the last five words correct. Try to join them with the first three—*sastik, mastic, kulik,*" stated one of the guide helpers.

"*Sastik, mastic, kulik, pelik, skeber, veber, milip, tips,*" Willie meowed loudly. He looked over his shoulder and let out a shriek as the big, beautiful wings appeared on his back.

"Calm down, Willie," the guide helper told him. "Now comes the fun part! The first lesson will be the takeoff, followed by a short flight low in the air, and then a landing. Let's begin with you, Minka," he directed, leaping over to the back of my angel cloud. "Come and join me."

I hesitantly trotted over to where he was standing. I was careful not to let my wings move, as I didn't want to break them.

"Relax, Minka," he said, smiling. "Your wings are extremely durable and flexible—they won't break. Now, run a few feet and say *brastik, astik.* That will get your wings to begin flapping and carry you into the air. To land, point all four of your paws downward. It's very simple."

I was nervous but did as I was told. I leaped forward, leaped again, and said, "*Brastic, astik.*"

Nothing happened.

"You need to run, not leap. And say the words with much more enthusiasm," meowed the guide helper.

I went back to the edge of my cloud, ran forward, and meowed loudly, "*Brastic, astik!*"

I felt my wings start to flutter and lift me up into the air. Instantly I was frightened. *Now what am I supposed to do?* I thought. As quickly as I went up, I flopped back down onto my angel cloud. I was startled and looked back at my wings to make sure that I had not ruined them. But they were in perfect condition.

"Don't scare yourself, or your wings," the guide helper reminded me gently. "Remember that your wings are getting used to you, just as you are getting used to them. Your wings need to

feel that you are in balance so they can balance you. Remember, point your paws downward for a safe landing."

I trotted to the edge of my cloud, turned, and ran forward. With much gusto I yelped, "*Brastic, astik!*"

I was lifted into the air and flew a few yards forward. I then pointed all my paws downward for a safe landing at the other edge of my cloud. "I think I did it!"

"Yes, you did!" all four guide helpers replied in unison. Then they leaped over to Willie's angel cloud. "Now it's your turn."

"I can do it, I can do it!" exclaimed Willie. He began leaping from one end of his angel cloud to the other, yelping, "*Brastic, brastic, brastic!*" He didn't seem to notice that he hadn't lifted off his angel cloud so much as an inch. "I can fly!"

The four guide helpers looked at one another and sighed.

"This will be enough for one night," one of them said. "Just say the eight magical words to remove your wings from your backs."

Willie and I did as we were told. Our wings magically disappeared and landed in front of the four guide helpers. They quickly gathered up our wings and flew off into the darkness, with a loud *rat-ta-ta* flapping sound that faded into the night.

"Did you see me fly?" exclaimed Willie. "I was really good. I can't wait until tomorrow night when I get to fly again!"

I smiled to myself. "You did great, Willie." Then I yawned, curled up on my angel cloud, and fell fast asleep.

The next night the guide helpers focused most of their attention on helping Willie learn to fly. At the beginning, his attempts were not successful, yet Willie felt sure he was flying. Even though the guide helpers were getting a bit frustrated, they didn't show it to Willie. They just patiently kept repeating the steps over and over again.

And then, all of a sudden, it clicked! As Willie loudly meowed the magical words, he rose up in the air. Once he was up, he pointed all four paws down to land at the tip of his angel cloud. Squealing in ecstasy, Willie repeated these steps several times before the guide helpers called it a night.

On the last night, the guide helpers taught us how to maneuver our wings while suspended in the air. We learned that we needed to twitch our right ear to turn right, and our left ear to turn left. We learned how to make circles by flicking our tails. To dive we had to point our heads down, and lift our heads higher to fly upwards. We even learned how to make somersaults in the air by curling up as though we were going to sleep.

Willie was much more daring than I was when it came to flying. He had a lot of natural speed and felt calm and at home in the air. He was as fast and agile as a seagull. He did somersaults all around me. I was naturally more cautious.

"Tomorrow night we will be taking a special trip to a cloud near the Angel Castle," one of the guide helpers told us. "Chloe and Oscar will meet us there, and the Angel Leaders will watch the two of you fly from their computer screens at the Angel Castle."

"Your ability to fly will determine whether the Angel Leaders approve your Earthly wish," another guide helper announced. Then all four flew off, making their loud *rat-ta-ta* flapping sound and carrying with them our beautiful, glowing wings.

Willie looked at me and took a nervous breath. I, too, felt a bit scared, yet I knew that this was a test we had to take if we were going to make our Earthly wish come true.

"We can do it—we can fly!" exclaimed Willie.

"I know we can," I promised as I nudged his head and licked his ears.

7. Test Flight

When midnight came, only two of the guide helpers appeared at our angel clouds. One of them grabbed onto Willie by the scruff of the neck and, with a loud *rat-ta-ta* of wings, began to fly north in the direction of the Angel Castle.

The other guide helper did the same with me, and we quickly followed behind Willie and his guide helper. I may have been a mellow cat on Earth, but I was thrilled! Since it was dark, I could not see clearly below us; I could just make out this and that. There were miles and miles of angel clouds, and every cloud had a cat sleeping on it. I hadn't realized how large Cat Heaven was! All the cats looked very peaceful, sleeping in their angel clouds. From high in the air I could see that a magical glowing fog surrounded every cloud, and realized that our angel clouds must glow as well.

We traveled on, leaving the part of Cat Heaven that housed the angel cats. All around me I could see only glowing mist. It was night, yet it seemed to be only dusk, like a summer night when

47

the sun hasn't fully set. As we flew through the fog, I had to keep my eyes closed some of the time because the glowing lights were so bright. But high in the air, I could sense a peaceful and magical force creating harmony and balance in every movement we made. Cats usually have a strong sixth sense, but this was a greater force than I'd ever experienced during my time on Earth.

Off in the distance I could see a large shimmering castle sitting on top of a radiant magical cloud. This must be the Angel Castle. It was made up of numerous scratching posts all linked together. Each scratching post was painted a vibrant hue and was encircled by shimmering stars of the same color. One was purple and violet, another blue and turquoise, a third teal and green, a fourth red and orange, and the last pink and fuchsia. The large central cat post was the brightest of all: it was colored a bright yellow, and from its multicolored rays, golden sparkles flickered through the air. A large golden wall encircled the Angel Castle and led to a big golden door.

We landed on a large white cloud a few yards away from the gates of the Angel Castle. Waiting for us were Chloe and Oscar and the other two guide helpers who had built our wings. We could see our finished wings assembled and ready to be attached.

"You two have had a remarkable journey," Chloe announced, whisking her tail back and forth. "During my time here, I have never known any angel cat—let alone two cats—who have come this far before completing their Earthly wish in the first phase of Cat Heaven. It is truly amazing."

We were silent. Then Oscar added, purring, "Your wings are beautiful."

"You will both need to show the Angel Leaders that you can fly. They want absolute perfection. No mistakes—otherwise it's a no-go," Chloe reminded us sternly. "There cannot be any uncertainty

that you'll be able to reach Earth or return to Cat Heaven."

I could see that Chloe looked tense. During the past few days, while our wings were being built, she seemed to become even more stern and demanding. I wasn't sure whether she was stressed at having to fulfill a very challenging Earthly wish or envious at our having the chance to fly to Earth again. When I thought about it, I realized it must be the first explanation. As far as I could tell, no negative emotions were allowed in Cat Heaven.

"Minka will go first. The Angel Leaders will be watching on large computer screens in the castle. They will closely watch your takeoff, flying ability, maneuvering, and landing," Oscar told me.

Bright lights suddenly appeared on the large cloud where we were standing.

"You will be judged on these four points. If the Angel Leaders have any doubt about your test flight, they will replay it in slow motion. They will review any point in question to determine your ability to fly. It is really important that you are able to fly without a problem," Oscar said. I could see he looked anxious.

Two perfect lines of golden lights appeared on the cloud. "This is your runway," Oscar explained, "where you will begin your test flight. Fly as high as you need in order to make a right turn, a left turn, and several circles, and then land at the very end of the runway."

Willie and I waited in silence. I was very nervous. I had no idea what Willie was feeling, but I knew he was paying attention.

"All right, Minka, let's go," exclaimed Chloe as her tail flicked back and forth.

I took a deep breath and trotted to the start of the runway. Then I turned to face Chloe, Oscar, and the four guide helpers. Finally I looked over at Willie, who was nudging his paws in the cloud. He gave me a smile.

"*Sastik, mastic, kulik, pelik, skeber, veber, milip, tips,*" I meowed as my wings magically appeared on my back. I stood for a moment and gazed at the runway, slightly moving my hips and back legs back and forth. I leaned forward into a run and meowed, "*Brastic, astik!*"

Quietly fluttering, my wings lifted me up into the air. I pointed my head up to make sure I had enough height before starting my first maneuver. First I turned to the right by twitching my right ear, and then I turned left by twitching my left ear. I pointed my head up to gain some more height. I flicked my tail and made two perfect circles. I completed my skills by curling up into a somersault. Finally I flew straight for a few yards before pointing my head down to begin my landing. With only a few feet to go, I pointed my paws downward for a perfect landing at the end of the runway.

"Excellent, Minka!" exclaimed Chloe. "You have such grace when you fly, and your moves were elegantly performed."

"Your turn, Willie," Oscar said as he quietly flapped his wings.

Bravely Willie took his stance at the start of the runway. He seemed amazingly calm and focused.

"*Sastik, mastic, kulik, pelik, skeber, veber, milip, tips,*" Willie meowed, and then turned to see his wings magically appear on his back.

He gazed at the runway and then at me. Dashing quickly, he exclaimed, "*Brastic, astik!*"

Immediately his wings began to flutter. He pointed his head up, and with a great deal of speed flew high into the air. He curled his body tightly and made several somersaults, and then pointed his left ear to make a sharp left turn and his right ear to make a quick right turn. He held his head upright to get more speed before flicking his tail to make two circles in the shape of a figure eight.

Then Willie lowered his head and with great speed flew downward, nearly touching the runway. But instead of landing, he quickly lifted his head again and whooshed into the air while tightly curling his body to make three somersaults in a row! Finally, Willie slowed his speed and positioned his head downward for his landing. He pointed all four paws and touched down at the end of the runway before trotting over to me. Excited, I licked his head again and again.

"Wow!" exclaimed Oscar.

The four guide helpers meowed and looked pleased, knowing they had done a very good job of teaching Willie how to fly.

"My, my. I never expected that from you, Willie," Chloe said. She seemed totally amazed. "You're a real natural in the sky!"

Together Willie and I chanted the magical code, and our wings disappeared from our backs and landed in front of the four guide helpers.

"The Angel Leaders will make a decision about your flying ability in the next few days. Go back to your angel clouds and get some rest, and Oscar and I will let you know whether your wish is a go," Chloe said as her tail twitched back and forth.

The two guide helpers who had brought us to this special cloud gripped us by the backs of our necks, and with the loud *rat-ta-ta* of their wings, they flew us back in the direction of our angel clouds. This time I was too tired to notice the glowing clouds above or below me. The flapping of their wings lulled me to sleep. Before I knew it, Willie and I were tucked in our cat beds on our angel clouds, falling into a very deep sleep.

8. The Decision

The next morning, I slowly awoke, yawned, and stretched. I recalled the night before and thought it was all a dream until I looked over at Willie's angel cloud. Then I felt my muscles twitch as though my wings were still on my back and realized that it wasn't a dream. Willie and I had actually gone to the Angel Castle to perform our test flights for the Angel Leaders!

I stretched my body to its full length and gazed up at the sky. I saw a remarkable shimmering light that gave me hope that Willie's and my Earthly wish would be granted.

"Willie, Willie . . ." I called softly.

Willie yawned and stretched his own body to its full length, and then looked over at me and quickly leaped into the air. He landed back on his cloud, nudged his paws into it, and flicked his tail before saying, "Wow, oh wow! We flew in front of the Angel Leaders last night!"

"We sure did," I happily answered.

"Do you think they will grant our wish?" Willie asked.

"I think that we have a pretty good chance, but I don't think we should feel too sure of ourselves. Our flying was awesome, true, but we don't know how the Angel Leaders judged it, particularly in terms of getting to Earth and back. We don't know which maneuver was most crucial to them."

"I think all four maneuvers were important, and you and I did a great job on all of them!" Willie responded.

Just then, Chloe arrived with a wonderful breakfast. She went about her regular business as if nothing had occurred the night before. Soon, Oscar appeared. Unlike Chloe, he couldn't conceal his excitement. He bounced all around Willie's angel cloud, asking if he needed any more food, treats, or water.

After breakfast, came bath time. The rest of the day was spent on our angel clouds, trying to remain calm by climbing trees, listening to birds and grasshoppers sing their tunes, cleaning our paws and fur, marking our territory by rubbing our noses, napping, and eating lunch and dinner until our bellies were full. We fell asleep early, exhausted from the night before as well as from waiting for news.

The next morning Chloe and Oscar appeared on our angel clouds. It was exactly two weeks to the day from when the guide helpers began building our wings. Rather than waking us with the usual morning routine, they just sat in front of us and waited until we were awakened by the soft fluttering sound of their wings.

I stretched and looked up at Chloe.

"Willie, Willie, time to get up," I purred softly.

Willie turned around a few times and stretched, and then looked at Oscar and leaped into the air. As soon as he landed back on his cloud, Chloe switched her tail back and forth and began to speak. "The Angel Leaders reviewed your test flights. Minka, although your circles were well rounded, the leaders were concerned about your height and speed before you actually performed the maneuver. In some circumstances, you would have been too low to make a complete circle, and you might have had an accident midair."

My heart sank to my stomach, and my tail whooshed back and forth. I kept looking at Chloe. I didn't dare look at Willie, knowing he must feel disappointed too. I couldn't bear to see his sad eyes. I was upset that I might have let Willie down.

Chloe went on with her report. "Willie, the Angel Leaders were concerned that you may have been too reckless with your flying, particularly during the last maneuver when you zoomed into the air to make three somersaults in a row. That was dangerous, and could have caused a bad collision."

I could tell Willie was very upset. He put his head down and began kneading his angel cloud.

"But . . ." Oscar began.

Willie and I looked up quickly.

"Despite their concerns, the Angel Leaders felt that you both demonstrated excellent flying ability. They have decided to grant you your Earthly wish to return to Earth to help your friends!" Oscar finished, fluttering over to Willie and nudging his head.

Willie began to squeal. Then Oscar and Willie raced in circles around his angel cloud, chanting, "Boy, oh, boy—wow, oh, wow!"

I just looked at Chloe. She was smiling at me.

"Thank you, Chloe," I said, "for helping to make this dream come true."

"It wasn't me, Minka, it was Willie and you. You were

determined to learn how to fly and did remarkably well," Chloe answered. "I've never known an angel cat to ask for such an outrageous Earthly wish or show this kind of zeal and perseverance. You not only believed in yourself, but you helped your friend, Willie, to stay focused and learn that with patience and hard work, a dream can become reality."

I purred and kneaded my angel cloud.

Chloe turned to Oscar and Willie, who were trampling all over Willie's angel cloud. "All right, you two," she shouted. "We still have a lot of work before you make your first trip to Earth."

The two of them screeched to a halt, ears cocked forward.

"Minka and Willie, you need to decide which four cats you plan to visit and why they need your attention. That is, which cat you will visit first, and the order of the three that follow. Oscar and I will return tomorrow to approve your decision. Let's go, Oscar," Chloe said. Then she fluttered above my cloud and turned north in the direction of the Angel Castle.

Oscar followed, but before he headed north, he swooshed back to nudge our heads. "I am so proud of you guys!" he called, and then flew off toward the Angel Castle.

Willie seemed frozen in amazement until I called him back to reality. "So, what friend do you want to visit first?"

"Casper!" Willie exclaimed.

"That might be a good choice. But first let's think about the other three cats who need our help. Then we can decide whether to visit Casper first. You know he is very independent and likes to do things his way. It may take a lot of work," I explained to Willie. "Come on, let's make a list."

"Casper and Muris!" Willie suggested as he leaped over to my angel cloud.

"Why do they need our help?" I asked, licking my paws.

"Hmm, well, Casper is always running outside and playing outdoors," Willie said. "He doesn't listen when he's called to come home, and sometimes he stays outside all night."

"Yes, we know the trouble you got into when you stayed outside," I reminded him.

"Yeah, I got real sick." Willie looked sad as he kneaded my angel cloud. "Or Casper could run into another animal when he is outside and not have anyone to help him."

"Casper needs to learn to stay in the comfort of his own home and not get into trouble roaming around outdoors," I agreed. "Muris, on the other hand, needs to learn to be nice to other cats and animals. He might be easier to help because he has mellowed in his old age."

"How about Muris first, then Casper to follow?" Willie said.

"Good. Now, Sofia should be the third cat we visit. Remember, she lived with you and Casper for several years, and then later with Muris and me. During the time she lived with you, she was the queen of the house and ate all the food that Anna placed in your food dish for the three of you. She got big and round," I reminded Willie, who nodded in agreement. "When she moved to our house, Muris wouldn't let her eat all the food, and she lost weight. She looks fine, but during my last year on Earth, she turned out to have diabetes."

"What's that?" Willie meowed.

"Sometimes Sofia has too much sugar in her bloodstream. Valerie gives her medicine twice a day and a good diet to control it and get rid of the extra sugar," I explained. "That's why she needs our help. If she doesn't stay on her diet, she could get really sick. We need to help her to eat right."

"We sure do!" Willie exclaimed. "Any idea who our fourth cat should be?"

We sat on my angel cloud, trying to figure out who our final friend in need could be. We discussed all the cats we'd known during our time on Earth, but we couldn't think of a cat who truly needed our help.

Feeling anxious, I began licking my paws intensely. If we couldn't come up with a fourth cat, our Earthly wish might not be granted. Chloe had specifically stated that we had to select four cats to protect on Earth, and that each must have a real need for our guidance.

"Aha!" I shouted. Startled, Willie leaped into the air and came tumbling down next to me.

"There was a beautiful young cat who moved into the neighborhood during my last few months on Earth. She was a little different from the rest. Not because of how she looked—in fact, she was lovelier than any of us. But I think she came from a faraway place, because she meowed a little differently. When I napped in the backyard, I often heard the other cats imitate her meows and laugh at her. Later I could hear her crying. I think she might need us to help the other cats realize that she is no different than they are and, in fact, has beautiful qualities that she can teach them."

"I remember her! She was pure gray," purred Willie. "But you're right, that wasn't nice to make fun of her just because she sounded different. I remember now. Her name was Zarah." Willie looked at me. "We have our four cats to visit!"

"We certainly do," I yawned, as we snuggled together for our afternoon nap.

It turned out to be a very long nap, extending into the early hours of the next day.

"Hey, you two, time to get up," I heard Oscar say as he nudged Willie out of a deep sleep. The two of us yawned and stretched. Then we looked up and saw Chloe and Oscar peering down at us.

Chloe looked annoyed that the two of us had slept on the same cloud. She always insisted that Willie go back to his own angel cloud at night. "Do you have a list for us?" she asked sternly as she fluttered about, getting my morning bath ready.

"Yes, we do. Willie, go ahead and tell Chloe and Oscar about the four cats we have chosen to visit on Earth."

Willie sat up and began to recite our list. "First, we will visit Muris and teach him how to be nice to other cats and animals. Next is Casper, who needs our help to learn to stay at home and not wander outside where he could be in danger or get sick. Sofia is the third cat we will visit. We plan to help her eat a better diet so she doesn't have so much sugar in her body. Our fourth cat is Zarah. She needs our help in teaching the other cats that she is the same as they are, even though her meows sound a little different."

Chloe smiled at Willie. I felt very impressed as well with his brief recital of our list.

"That's a great list!" Oscar exclaimed.

"Approved!" Chloe chimed in. "Which means that tonight you will go on your first visit to help Muris. The guide helpers and both of us will arrive at your angel clouds at midnight to wish you a safe journey."

"I have a question," I spoke up. "How do we know the direction to Earth, and Muris's house?"

Chloe chuckled. "Now you know why I had to approve the list of cats you planned to visit on Earth. This way, the Angel Leaders can have their assistants look up their addresses on the Felinequest website and imprint the directions on your wings. Don't forget, you still need to take off, land, and turn when you visit Earth," Chloe explained as she and Oscar fluttered above our angel clouds. "Get some rest before midnight," she added, her voice trailing off in the air as the two flew away toward the horizon.

Chloe always knew what I was thinking; I guess that's why she was my angel buddy. I winked at Willie to get back on my angel cloud so that we could play for the remainder of the day and then get in a long nap before our midnight summons.

Part Two—Earth

9. Muris

At precisely midnight, Chloe, Oscar, and the four guide helpers appeared carrying our beautiful wings. (I had made sure that Willie went back to his angel cloud about an hour before midnight.)

We were ready to go, though I felt nervous and my stomach was tied in knots. I was sure Willie had butterflies flying around inside his tummy too. I couldn't believe the two of us would soon be flying back to Earth, and that I would soon see Muris, my very best friend and partner in life. I kept imagining what it would be like to feel the Earth's air again, smell the scents, and see my old home where Muris and I used to play and sleep, as well as see Valerie again. It was Valerie who cradled me as I passed from my Earth life to the Heavenly World. It all seemed surreal, yet soon I would be in my Earth's life again, experiencing everything I missed about Earth.

"I have a few important instructions," Chloe announced.

Willie and I stood upright on our clouds. "First, time is experienced on Earth very differently than in Cat Heaven. In order to complete all three visits to each cat you have chosen to help, you will need to travel down to Earth nearly every night. A few days off here and there and between cats have been worked into your schedule," Chloe meowed.

Willie and I nodded in assent.

"That doesn't mean it will be nighttime on Earth or only a day or two since your last visit. Sometimes several days will have passed, and at other times a week or even a month," instructed Chloe. "There is no rhyme or reason to the way time travels between Earth and Cat Heaven. You must trust the laws of Higher Cat Heaven that you will be placed on Earth at exactly the perfect time."

Again, Willie and I nodded in unison.

Chloe went on. "Remember, no visit may go beyond four hours. If you pass the time limit during any of the visits, that cat won't learn anything from you," she explained. "Each of you will be given a golden cat watch to keep track of time during these visits. Your watches will meow loudly when there are fifteen minutes left and again when you have ten minutes left, five minutes left, and finally one minute remaining before the visit must end."

Willie and I placed the golden watches on our left front paws.

"Finally, if you get in trouble—"

"Trouble!" exclaimed Willie. His tail lashed back and forth worriedly.

"No," Oscar blurted, "not the way you get in trouble with us. She means if you need our help in any way."

Oscar smiled. "Here is a special Heavenly iPhone. Just use your toes to dial the words 'cat heaven'—two-two-eight, four-three-two-eight-three-six."

"Oh, wow!" exclaimed Willie.

"I'm going to let Minka wear the iPhone, but Willie can use it too." Oscar clipped the iPhone on my cat collar. Then he nodded. It was time to go.

"*Sastik, mastic, kulik, pelik, skeber, veber, milip, tips,*" I meowed, and my wings magically appeared on my back.

Willie immediately followed my command. "*Sastik, mastic, kulik, pelik, skeber, veber, milip, tips!*"

"Remember, your wings will have imprinted directions that will get you to Muris's home," Oscar advised. "However, you must maneuver your own wings once you land on Earth."

Chloe was pacing my angel cloud with her tail held straight in the air. "Before you take off, I have one last gift to give you." With her mouth, she nudged her collar around and then tugged and pulled off a golden packet. "This is filled with Heavenly golden dust. It's magic. The Heavenly dust will do anything. But I must warn you, there is only a small portion for each of your four friends, so you must use it only when you really need to."

Willie and I nodded. Chloe carefully placed the packet of golden dust around my collar. "Wear it at all times," she instructed. "Do not take the pack off your collar even while you are in Cat Heaven. Now have a safe flight!"

I gazed up at the sky, and then looked over at Willie. He was standing in his preflight position: front legs slightly bent, head and chest forward, ready to go!

We both ran forward, exclaiming, "*Brastic, astik!*" and fluttered into the air. Our angel wings quickly whooshed to the left, and then, as fast as the speed of light, we felt ourselves descend through the fresh ozone layer of the Heavenly World and into the Earth's atmosphere.

We traveled for miles and miles, all the while descending. The sky was getting lighter. I looked down at Earth for landmarks, but we were traveling too fast to make out any of the land below.

Once again, our angel wings whooshed us to the left, then down through fluffy white clouds. We were approaching a town. As we drew closer, I realized it was the beautiful city of Seattle, where I had lived most of my life. I could not believe it! We were flying high above the city. I could see the Space Needle, the waterfront with ferries traveling to and from the San Juan Islands, even the two bridges across Lake Washington. As we descended, we traveled north along the interstate. Finally, I saw our neighborhood—Willie's and my Earthly homes, next to each other, separated by a tall wooden fence. Oh, how I missed my home.

Before we knew it, we had landed inside my old bedroom. The orange-and-green cat bed where Muris and I used to sleep was still next to Valerie's bed, and our matching green food and water dishes were placed in the same spots near the bathroom door. I felt as though I had been there yesterday. Nothing had changed. No one was in the bedroom, and no cat or dog was in sight.

"Minka, we're in your house," Willie whispered. He gazed around in total amazement. "What should we do now?"

I looked at my old bedroom and thought about all the sweet memories that this place held for me. I wanted to leap into my old bed and curl up for a long afternoon nap, but that was not why I was here.

"Maybe we should try to find Muris."

"That's a good idea," whispered Willie.

We started to tiptoe toward the open door leading to the hallway. I peered around the door and saw Muris lounging in the middle of the hall. Startled, I leaped back, nearly knocking Willie to the ground.

"Hey, why'd you do that?" he complained.

"Shh! I just saw Muris in the hallway!"

"Should we just go up and say hello?" Willie asked.

"I feel a little nervous seeing him again," I remarked as my tail twitched back and forth.

We peered around the door again. Muris was busy grooming himself. Even though he was nearly eighteen years old, twice the age that most cats live, he was as handsome as ever. He had a very distinguished look due to his tuxedo markings—a lustrous gray coat, a white goatee, and markings on his chest, stomach, and paws.

A flood of emotions soared through my heart. I was so happy to see him, yet sad that I was no longer with him on Earth. He had always been so good to me. I missed his warmth, his nudges on my face, and his licks around the ears. I missed eating with him, lounging throughout the day, and sleeping with him at night. We had spent sixteen years together, which in cat time was over a century.

Willie and I tiptoed slowly along the hallway, and then leaped over Muris and landed in front of him. He sneezed but didn't seem to notice us. He kept on grooming.

"Hey, Muris," Willie meowed, "it's Willie!"

Muris just sneezed again. Instead of saying hello, he finished grooming and got up to head down the hall toward the kitchen. On the way, he walked right through the two of us and sneezed again.

Pointing our ears to the left, Willie and I flew to the kitchen to watch Muris. He approached Lana, the beautiful German shepherd, who was drinking from her water bowl. Muris walked over and swatted her on the nose. Startled, Lana moved aside, and Muris began drinking water out of her bowl.

I felt baffled. Muris had always been the dominant cat in the household, but this aggressive behavior toward Lana was new.

After he finished drinking water from the dog's bowl, Muris wandered to the dining room. Willie and I pointed our ears right and fluttered over to watch his next move.

Slowly Muris approached Sofia, who was lounging by the sliding glass door, enjoying the warmth of the afternoon sun. I felt a pang when I looked at her dear tiger-cat face. But I knew this wasn't the time to reminisce about Sofia. There would be different visits planned for her.

I looked back at Muris. At that moment, he swatted Sofia on the nose. Sofia quickly got up and retreated to the living room area as Muris took her warm spot near the glass door.

"Muris!" Willie exclaimed. "That's not very nice!"

Muris sneezed again. He seemed to look directly at the spot where Willie hovered.

"I think he can see you, Willie!" I remarked excitedly. "Let me try and talk some sense into him."

I positioned myself in front of Muris. "Muris, it's Minka. I must say, I am totally surprised at your behavior!"

For a second, he stared right at me. He then looked around the room, scratched his ears, licked his paws, and finally curled into a ball for a nap.

I sighed with frustration. I wasn't getting through to Muris. "He can't see or hear us, Willie." Chloe had said that Muris might not be able to see us until our final visit, but it still made me sad. "After so many years, I thought he would get a sense of me being around, like an angel watching over him."

Again, I ventured over to Muris. "I miss you so much," I whispered softly.

Muris's ears twitched slightly, and then he yawned and repositioned himself. I nudged his head; again, he repositioned himself. I licked his ears. Muris lifted his head, shook it slightly, and made a soft grunting noise.

I felt excited. I was making a connection with him!

The nearness of my old friend was too much to resist. Finally, I snuggled next to Muris and dozed off.

As I napped next to Muris, Willie decided to explore the house from an angel's-eye view. He had a great time running through the walls and the furniture. Willie leaped from one end of the room to the other and did a somersault before pointing his paws to make a perfect landing. Willie was a bit dismayed when he found he couldn't push cat toys or pick them up in his mouth, but he had a great time jumping over Lana and riding on her back. Whenever Willie rubbed his head in her fur, Lana would sneeze, bouncing him high in the air.

Suddenly I was awakened by a loud meow. It was coming from my cat watch.

"Oh, dear, we only have fifteen minutes left!" I exclaimed. "Willie, where are you?"

From the living room, Willie quickly pointed his ears to the left and fluttered over to me.

"We haven't accomplished much during this visit, and it's my fault," I meowed. "I was too wrapped up in seeing Muris again. I miss him so much."

"Things like this are bound to happen during our first visits," Willie reassured me. "Don't forget, we still have two more trips to visit Muris."

"Yes, and a lot of work to do." I felt nervous as I looked over at Muris, who was snuggled in his cozy nap mode.

There was another loud meow from our watches—ten minutes left.

Willie and I tiptoed back into the bedroom. We didn't wait for another signal before we shouted "*Brastic, astik!*"

Off we flew—through the house, the city, the fluffy white clouds, Earth's sky, the fresh ozone layer of the Heavenly World, and finally back to our angel clouds.

Our guide helpers were there to greet us after our first safe journey back to Cat Heaven. We chanted the magical eight-word code and saw our wings disappear from our backs and land in front of the four guide helpers. They flew off, making their loud *rat-ta-ta* flapping sound and carrying our beautiful, glowing wings for storage until our next visit to Earth.

But now that we had visited Muris once, I was beginning to feel unsure. There was no way my Earthly wish would be accomplished if we remained invisible. There must be something else I could try next time. But what?

10. The Flowerpot

The next morning, I didn't want to move from my angel cloud. I was so disappointed in my failure to contact Muris. I desperately needed to find a way to get through to him!

Chloe and Oscar appeared on our angel clouds to hear about our trip to Earth. But first, Oscar licked Willie all over to make sure he was all right after being so far away from Cat Heaven.

"Did you have any success with Muris?" Chloe asked.

"Some," I said, and curled up into a tight ball.

Chloe sensed my dismay. "Maybe before your next trip to Earth, you should come up with a plan about what you need to accomplish with Muris."

I nodded sadly.

"He changed after you left, Minka," Chloe said softly. "He really misses you, he is sad, and that may be why he is lashing out at Lana and Sofia. Since he can't hear you, perhaps there is another way to help him besides talking to him."

I turned to Chloe. "How did you know what happened during

73

our visit to Earth, and about what Muris might be feeling?"

"We know and see everything here in Cat Heaven," Chloe told me.

"I'm at a loss about what to do, and also worried that I will get so caught up in seeing him again that I'll lose track of time," I meowed.

"Think of how to use your powers—after all, you are an angel. You just need to focus."

I sat up and looked into Chloe's eyes.

"Your angel powers are at an infancy stage because you and Willie have not learned to tap into them," remarked Chloe. "If you want to move an object on Earth, then you need to really focus on that object and see the object moving. You may become really tired after using a certain power for the first few times or after using the power intensely, just like a kitten gets tired after play. But that feeling will go away the more you use that power."

I nodded at Chloe.

"The more comfortable the two of you become with being on Earth, the more you will have a sense of what needs to be done and how your powers may help you. Also, your powers will advance each time you travel to Earth. Now that does not mean you can do anything on Earth—there are limits, as you are young angel cats and only in the first phase of Cat Heaven."

"How about the heavenly dust you gave us?" I asked Chloe.

"Simply wish that it will do something for you, and it will." Chloe began pacing around my angel cloud with her tail upright. "But I must *caution* you to use the dust *wisely*. There is just enough heavenly dust for each of your friends."

Chloe's idea made me start thinking of a plan. I felt eager to fly down to Earth again and try to help Muris become a friendlier cat.

Midnight approached. As soon as Chloe, Oscar, and the guide helpers appeared, Willie and I shouted, "*Sastik, mastic, kulik, pelik, skeber, veber, milip, tips!*" Instantly our heavenly wings appeared on our backs.

Without hesitation, we ran forward and exclaimed, "*Brastic, astik!*" and fluttered into the air. Our angel wings whooshed us to the left, and again we descended through the fresh, clean ozone layer of the Heavenly World into the Earth's sphere. We traveled for miles before reaching the beautiful city of Seattle and our Earth homes.

As soon as we were inside the bedroom, I flew to where Muris was grooming himself after his morning meal. I pointed my head up and flew above him, and then pointed my ear to the left and flew into the kitchen. Willie followed behind.

Muris sneezed twice and stopped grooming. I focused on the water dish in the kitchen and pushed it with my paw. Willie meowed with excitement when the dish moved several inches.

"Wow, Minka, is the plan to scare Muris into becoming a friendlier cat?"

"Not much scares Muris, but we might get his attention so he realizes something different is going on," I answered.

"Here he comes!" Willie said excitedly, flicking his tail back and forth.

Slowly Muris walked over to the dish and began lapping up the water. I focused for a few seconds and then pushed the water dish away from him. Muris watched it move, and then looked back at the spot where the dish had been and again at the place it had stopped. He moved over to the dish and started drinking.

This time, with much concerted effort, I managed to push the dish several feet away from him. Water splashed all over Muris. Willie shrieked and leaped up. Muris sneezed, shook his head, and pawed the water off his face as Willie and I giggled. He stared at the water dish for a long time before finally retreating to the dining room. I followed closely behind.

Lana and Sofia both sat in the dining room. Their eyes were focused on the water dish in the kitchen. Lana's head was propped slightly to the left, and she barked several times. Sofia kept staring at the water dish with great intensity as her tail swooshed back and forth.

Muris walked over to them and then paused. He looked at Lana and swatted her twice on the nose. The dog let out a slight yelp. He tried to do the same with Sofia, but she darted into the living room.

"Muris!" I yelled. "Stop being unkind!"

Muris didn't react. He obviously couldn't hear me meow.

Meanwhile, Willie was experimenting with his new angel powers. He found a small catnip mouse behind the couch. Snatching the toy in his mouth, he twitched his ear to the left and fluttered over to where Muris was sitting. He dropped the toy in front of Muris and then moved it in a circle.

At first Muris tried to catch the mouse. He ran after it a few times, but before long he was bored with it. Muris didn't find anything unusual about a toy mouse trotting around in circles.

Willie spotted a scratching post near the sliding glass door. He pushed it over to where Muris was sitting. Muris calmly watched the post slowly move toward him. Perhaps his mellowed old age and distinguished stance in life made Muris feel that objects simply appeared when he needed them. He scratched the post a few times

and then looked out the sliding glass door. The door was open, and Muris went outside onto the deck.

I summoned Willie. We were both tired after moving objects for the first time, so we rested for a few minutes before joining Muris out on the deck.

"Ready?" We lifted our heads and flew after Muris, and then pointed our paws and made a perfect landing next to him.

It was a beautiful spring day. Several flowerpots were arranged on the deck railing. A large oak tree stood next to the house with its branches hanging down next to the flowerpots. I could hear birds singing in the tree.

Muris jumped onto one of the lounge chairs and curled into a ball for a catnap. I leaped onto the chair beside him to figure out our next move. Though I was determined to make progress, I was worried we were running out of time. Willie was having a blast flying from one end of the deck to the other, doing double somersaults in the air and landing on the grill, lounge chairs, and even the railing itself.

Suddenly, Muris's head popped up and he looked toward the giant oak tree. I looked over to see what had caught his attention. There was a bird's nest nestled in one of the branches, and inside were four baby birds chirping loudly as they waited for their mother's return. Muris ran to the far end of the deck and leaped onto the rail and over one of the flowerpots. He began to make a funny clicking noise with his mouth while his tail darted back and forth.

Muris was about to leap over another flowerpot to get closer to the birds when Willie's somersault brought him down on the flowerpot and knocked him to the ground. Willie pointed his head up quickly to gain speed and then somersaulted himself to the other side of the deck. He pointed his paws for a perfect landing.

Three loud cat meows sounded from my cat watch—fifteen minutes to go.

Muris jumped up, hissed at the flowerpot, and ran inside the house just as the mother bird appeared with food for her nestlings.

As I watched the mother bird feed her chicks, I suddenly realized what we needed to do.

There was another loud meow from our watches—ten minutes left.

Willie flew over to me. "Sorry that I scared Muris back into the house."

"On the contrary—your timing was impeccable. And you gave me the perfect idea."

One more meow—we only had five minutes left.

"What is it?" Willie exclaimed.

"Not now. We need to return to Cat Heaven, and if we don't leave now, Muris will learn nothing. I'll explain it to you after we get a good night's sleep," I told him, still staring at the mother bird.

We trotted forward and shouted, *"Brastic, astik!"* Off we flew through the city of Seattle and the Earth's sky. As we flew into the fresh ozone layer of the Heavenly World and back to our angel clouds, I kept thinking about my plan to help Muris. Even though Muris usually had his own plan, my plan could outsmart him. I felt a rush of excitement flutter through my soul.

The guide helpers were there to greet us when we landed. We chanted the magical eight-word code, and our wings disappeared to be carried off by the four guide helpers. They flew off into the distance, making their loud *rat-ta-ta* flapping sound and carrying our beautiful glowing wings.

Willie and I fell asleep as soon as our heads hit our angel pillows.

The next morning, we were already waiting when Chloe and Oscar showed up to hear about our second trip to Earth. Oscar again licked Willie from head to toe, checking to make sure he was all right.

"How did it go?" Chloe inquired.

"We were able to get Muris's attention this time. We irritated him by moving his water dish. Then Willie knocked over the flowerpot, startling Muris while he was stalking some baby birds in the nest," I explained.

"That's great progress. But you only have one more trip to help Muris become a better cat, and I'm not sure how you are going to help him," Chloe meowed as she leaped onto Willie's cloud.

"I have a plan," I stated confidently as my tail twitched back and forth.

"Okay, then. The two of you need your rest for your final flight to Earth to help Muris. Oscar and I will return at midnight."

As soon as they left, I told Willie of my plan. I was sure it would teach Muris to become a friendlier cat without distressing him, which was important given Muris's old age. I explained when Willie should move the water dish and leap, and where to make his somersault landings. He excitedly agreed to all my instructions. Still, I didn't dare explain the final move, partly because I wasn't completely sure how it would work myself.

As we waited for our final trip, I told myself that where there was a Willie, there was a way.

11. Mother Bird

Midnight arrived. As soon as Chloe, Oscar, and the guide helpers appeared, Willie and I quickly shouted, *"Sastik, mastic, kulik, pelik, skeber, veber, milip, tips!"* Our heavenly wings instantly appeared on our backs.

We ran forward, exclaimed, *"Brastic, astik!"* and fluttered up into the air.

Our angel wings quickly whooshed us to the left, and we descended downward through the ozone layer of the Heavenly World into the Earth's sphere. Before descending into Seattle, I was in deep concentration about our last visit to help Muris. I was excited yet nervous about my plan, and about how Muris would react to seeing me if it worked.

Before I knew it, we were inside the bedroom. The two of us fluttered over to the dining room, where Muris was grooming himself, and stood right next to him. I told Willie this was no time to play around; we had to remain focused. Luckily, Lana and Sofia were nowhere in sight. I was worried their presence would distract Muris.

I heard noise in the kitchen. I quickly fluttered over to the entrance of the kitchen and saw Valerie pouring coffee into her mug. A wave of loving emotions tingled through my angel soul. Oh, how I missed Valerie's touch, hugs, and kisses, and wished I could feel them again. Valerie gathered her mug and work bag and walked down the stairs and out the front door. As much as I wanted to follow Valerie, Willie and I were on our last visit to help Muris and I could not allow any diversions. Plus, it was good that Valerie would not be around the house. She would see that strange things were happening and derail my plan.

I moved over to the sliding glass door.

"Oh, dear!" I exclaimed. The sliding door was closed. We needed to get Muris out on the deck for my plan to work!

Willie quickly flew over. I was surprised at his intensity; he immediately started clawing at the door. After a few minutes of clawing at the bottom of the door and then at the side, Willie was able to move it slightly.

"I can open it," Willie panted. "It may tire me out, but I can do it!"

The door was heavy. I knew that Willie wouldn't be able to do all the moves I needed him to do on the deck if he was exhausted, but it was critical to get Muris outside.

"Go for it," I told him, "and I will help you as best as I can." I licked his ear for reassurance.

Willie stared at the sliding door for a few seconds and then again pounced down and began clawing at the side of the door. He was able to push it just enough to get both paws through the open crack. Using all his angel power, he clawed and clawed and was able to push the sliding door open a few more inches.

He flopped down. "I need to rest a bit, and then I can try some more," he gasped.

"You've done great, Willie. I'll do the rest."

Willie had done all that he could. There was just enough space in the opening for Muris to squeeze through, but I needed a way to make Muris want to go outdoors.

I focused and then pounced into the same position as Willie. By clawing at the door, I was able to push it open enough for Muris to get a scent of the fresh air and roam out onto the deck. I, too, was fatigued and wasn't sure how much more angel power I had to carry out the rest of my plan. I lay down next to Willie to catch my breath.

Muris had been watching as the door opened ever so slightly, just enough for him to venture outdoors. He didn't seem alarmed that the door had opened on its own accord. In fact, he made a grunting sound and headed onto the deck with his tail twitching back and forth.

Willie and I were so tired that we were unable to move as Muris walked right through us. He sneezed and then jumped onto the lounge chair, where he curled into a ball for his midmorning nap.

"Willie," I said. "We have to keep moving. Otherwise our time will run out, along with our Earthly wish."

Willie nodded, and we dragged ourselves out to the deck and flopped down next to the lounge chair. I gazed up at the oak tree where I'd seen the bird's nest. The four baby birds were chirping loudly as they awaited their mother's return.

I thought quickly. "Willie, I need you to jump onto the ledge of the deck. Forget about all the moves I told you to do. As soon as you see the mother bird flying toward the nest, can you make a somersault and bump the mother bird—just enough to startle her?"

With my remaining strength, I jumped to the top of the railing. "I will watch over Muris to make sure he doesn't attempt a lunge toward the nest before the mother arrives."

"Minka, I need more running speed and height before I can make a somersault," Willie said.

"Okay, go to the far end of the deck. Keep your eyes glued on the nest and tree. When you see the mother bird flying toward them, make your move just before she lands," I told him.

Slowly Willie wobbled down to the end of the deck. He was still exhausted from sliding the dining room door open. I wasn't sure whether he had enough strength to run, let alone fly, do his somersault move, and make a perfect landing in the bird's nest. To make matters worse, I didn't know if I had the strength to keep Muris from getting to the bird's nest before the mother bird arrived.

Using all my angel powers, I concentrated on the whereabouts of the mother bird. She was traveling back to the nest over several nearby rooftops. As I moved one of the flowerpots to make it easy to land on the deck, the sound startled Muris. He looked up and then spotted the bird's nest.

Within a second, he was over at the far end of the deck. Muris leaped onto the rail over my head, sneezed, and positioned himself close to the nest. He made a funny clicking noise with his mouth while his tail darted back and forth.

I nearly fell off the railing as I fumbled for the packet of golden dust around my collar. I tugged at the sack with my mouth to open it and managed to get a small portion of dust on my right paw as I struggled to keep my balance.

When I looked up, I saw the mother bird approaching.

Muris jumped toward the nest. I leaped into the air to intercept him. I landed and wobbled on the branch next to the nest. Holding the golden dust, I shouted, "Now, Willie, now!" just as Muris tumbled down to the deck.

Willie's wings fluttered into action. He pointed his head upward and, with as much speed as he could muster, raised himself into the air. Tightly curling his body, he made a large somersault. Then he pointed all four paws and touched down on the bird's nest, slightly bumping into the startled mother bird.

As Willie fluttered into the air, I opened my paw and sprinkled the bird with golden dust. Then I made my wish.

Immediately she fluttered toward Muris and knocked him several times on the tip of his nose. She then retreated to her nest.

I saw that Muris's nose was bleeding where he'd been pecked. Meowing with pain, he ran into the house.

I waved at Willie to follow. The two of us flew into the dining room, where Muris was pawing his nose to try to stop the bleeding. He meowed several times and flicked his tail back and forth. Then he spotted Lana lounging in the living room. He ran over and stared into her eyes. Expecting a swat from Muris, she was about to get up and leave her spot when she hesitated and looked at him.

Instead of swatting her, Muris nudged her. He did this several times and began to purr. Looking grateful, Lana licked his nose before retreating to her sleeping den. The fur on Muris's coat began to take on a beautiful glow.

Next, Muris sought out Sofia. He spotted her behind the living room couch. She, too, began to run away instinctively, but

then, just as Lana had, she turned to face Muris. Softly he nudged her head. Sofia meowed and licked Muris's nose and around his ears. The bleeding stopped. She moved closer, purred, and lay beside him. As Muris cushioned himself next to her, Sofia rested her head on his back.

I felt excited. Muris must have realized that the pain from the mother bird's pecks was like the pain Lana and Sofia felt from his swats. Muris felt bad. He was hurting deep inside. He missed me, and because of his own hurt, he tried to hurt others. But hopefully not anymore.

Loud meows came from my cat alarm watch—fifteen minutes to go.

Sofia heard the strange noise and ran into the bedroom. Muris also heard it. He stood up as Willie and I flew to the living room and stood in front of him. A beautiful translucent light engulfed the entire room. Golden sparkles shimmered in the air as Willie and I magically appeared in front of Muris. Our wings glistened with radiant colors.

Muris's eyes opened wide as he stared at us. "My gosh," he whispered, "is it you, Minka? Are you really here? You look so beautiful."

"Yes, Muris, it's me," I answered softly, rustling my wings. "Willie's here too."

Willie fluttered into the air and did a figure eight. Muris watched Willie in amazement and then looked back at me.

"You look like an angel with those bright, colorful wings," he said.

"I am an angel," I told him, opening my wings wide. "Willie and I came down from Cat Heaven to help you become a friendlier cat," I said.

"Cat Heaven—is there such a place?"

"Yes, it's where we go after our time on Earth. It's not much different than Earth, except that everything is peaceful, bright, and beautiful," I explained. "We watch over our cat friends from Cat Heaven."

"Will I go there too?" Muris wanted to know.

"Yes, when your time comes to join us, you will," I assured him.

"But why are you here?" Muris asked.

"We were worried about you in Cat Heaven because you were swatting and hurting the other animals who live with you. After being your partner for so many years, I know you are not the friendliest cat. But lately you seem very sad," I told Muris. "That's not you. I wanted you to be happy again."

Muris put his head down. He let me nudge him and lick his ears.

When he looked up at me, his eyes were glazed with tears. "I can feel you, Minka," Muris said as he nudged my head and pawed at my wings.

"Yes, you can, and I can feel you," I answered as I licked his ears.

"I've missed you so much. I miss my morning meals with you, and playing and sleeping next to you. I didn't know what to do without you. Lana and Sofia aren't like you. I wanted them to go away," Muris said sadly. "But when the bird pecked me on the nose, I had to run to them for help. I realized they can be my friends. They may not be you, but they are on my side, to protect and love me."

"Yes, they are there for you," I said.

The cat meows from my cat watch startled Muris—they signaled ten minutes to go.

"Willie and I need to go back to Cat Heaven soon," I said softly.

"Will I ever see you again?" Muris asked.

"Not here on Earth, but when it is time to join us in Cat Heaven, we will live together forever," I explained.

"Now that I've seen you again, I might start to swat at Lana and Sofia again," Muris said. "I might start missing you even more."

"No, you won't," I told him firmly. "You have learned your lesson," I meowed.

My cat watch meowed too—five minutes left.

"The love I felt with you during my time on Earth is the same love I feel for you from Cat Heaven. It has not gone away, and it never will. I think of you every minute of every day. Only now, I live in your heart," I whispered in Muris's ear. "I will always be your angel watching over you."

"I love you, too, Minka. I guess the time I have on Earth will be more peaceful knowing you are my angel and will always be beside me," he said.

Willie and I stood in front of Muris. Our wings, with their thousands of bird feathers, opened wide. Each feather glowed, creating a tapestry of colors—yellow shining as bright as the sun's rays, red as rich as the color of roses, blue as serene and deep as the ocean, and gold shimmering magically.

As Muris watched in amazement, he briefly took on an angelic appearance.

"Until we meet again," I whispered.

"Until we meet again, Minka," Muris meowed.

Then the two of us shouted, *"Brastic, astik!"* Off we flew over the city of Seattle, into the Earth's sky, into the Heavenly World, and back to our angel clouds. I was mesmerized during the entire trip back to Cat Heaven, thinking of how surreal it was for Muris to see me in my angel form and how the love we shared had not changed. We would always be a part of each other. I would miss him every heavenly day until he joined me in Cat Heaven.

When we landed on our clouds, the guide helpers were there to greet us. We chanted our code, and our wings disappeared and landed in front of the four guide helpers. The guide helpers flew off into the distance carrying our beautiful, glowing wings.

Willie and I smiled at each other. We fell asleep as soon as our heads hit our angel pillows.

12. Casper

Willie and I slept for a very long time. I wasn't sure if it was late morning or mid-afternoon when Chloe and Oscar appeared at our angel clouds.

"It's time to wake up!" exclaimed Oscar. "We are very excited to hear about your final visit with Muris."

Oscar was fluttering over Willie's angel cloud to get him ready for the big meal he had prepared. Though Willie was famished, he jabbered with Oscar the whole time. Willie didn't leave out a detail of how we had helped Muris become a friendlier cat.

I yawned and stretched. Then I gazed at Chloe, who was flying over my cloud. She didn't say anything at first, but just prepared my breakfast. When I was done eating, Chloe began to bathe me. She lathered me with a lot of oils and soap. "The two of you have done very well," she remarked as she rinsed the soap from my fur. "Muris is a changed cat, enjoying his time with Lana and Sofia. He no longer swats them, but plays with them instead. He is content."

"So you saw everything that happened during our last visit?" I asked.

"Yes, we did," responded Chloe. "Now it's time to rest for a few days. You used a lot of your angel powers. You need time to recuperate and think about what to do with Casper."

I agreed. As soon as Chloe was finished drying me, I curled into a tight ball and fell asleep.

After a few days of rest and relaxation, I was getting anxious about our next visit to Earth. These were going to be about Casper, a cat I hadn't spent much time with during my life on Earth. It was Willie's idea to visit him. He felt Casper needed our help because he was always running outside and staying out all night.

"Willie, do you have any idea what we can do with Casper?" I kneaded his angel cloud and then trotted to the other end.

"We have to keep him from staying outdoors," responded Willie as he watched me nervously move around on his cloud.

"Do you have a plan?" I asked. "I hope so, since we are leaving for Earth at midnight."

"We'll figure that out when we get there," Willie said casually.

I didn't answer. Willie had been so excited about our success with Muris that I was worried he might think our Earthly missions would be easy from here on out.

Midnight arrived. As soon as Chloe, Oscar, and the guide helpers appeared, Willie and I quickly shouted, *"Sastik, mastic, kulik, pelik, skeber, veber, milip, tips!"* Our heavenly wings instantly appeared on our backs.

We both ran forward and exclaimed, *"Brastic, astik!"* and fluttered into the air.

Our angel wings quickly whooshed us to the left, through the fresh, clean ozone layer of the Heavenly World and into the Earth's sphere. As we descended into the beautiful city of Seattle and veered north along the interstate, I noticed the heavy car traffic. I thought that it must be morning, and that Valerie might even be caught up in it while making her way to work. She would often complain about the morning traffic on the interstate—now I realized what she was talking about. I would have complained too, if it were me!

Finally we arrived at Willie's Earth home. It was next to Muris's house, separated by a large brown fence. I wondered what Muris was doing. Then I remembered we had another mission to focus on, and that Muris was safe and loved in his home.

Willie and I fluttered around Casper's home. "Where do you think he might be?" I asked Willie, after licking a few of my wing feathers to straighten them out. "You two must have had regular sleeping spots around the house."

Willie wandered from one room to another. He looked under a bed, on top of some cat posts, by the water dish, on the living room couch, and in a hiding spot by a large plant, but he could not find Casper. "He's got to be here somewhere," he exclaimed.

I could tell Willie was getting anxious. "Let's try looking through the entire house. Then if we can't find him, we can go outdoors and look for him."

Willie fluttered around the house, carefully checking each favorite spot. Casper was nowhere to be found. "It's time to go outdoors," he announced.

As we ventured into the backyard, I gazed over at my old home and caught a glimpse of Muris and Sofia lounging on the deck. They were snuggled close together. I felt relieved.

"Let's go to the front yard," Willie suggested. "I'm sure we will find Casper there."

We twitched our ears to the right and pointed our heads upward. We flew over the roof and then pointed our paws down to make a safe landing in the front yard. Still, no Casper.

"Casper liked to wander down the street and around the neighborhood," meowed Willie. "Let's fly up the street and search around some of the nearby houses."

I said nothing, but I had a feeling this was going to be a difficult mission. We were spending most of our time searching for Casper. We hadn't even made contact with him, never mind come up with a plan for what we were going to do. Time was quickly running out.

Willie headed up the street and I quickly followed. He gazed around the neighborhood but could not find Casper. When we reached the end of the street, Willie suddenly pointed his right ear to make a quick right turn. "I found him!" he shouted.

That's when I saw Casper. He was a stunningly beautiful Siamese, pure white with calico markings. Casper was lean. His white tail was long, with the tip marked in calico. When he turned his head in our direction, I noticed his striking blue eyes.

"Let's approach to see where he might be headed," Willie instructed.

When we flew next to Casper, Willie got excited; he fussed over Casper, licking his ears and nudging his head. Casper only sneezed.

A half a block away I saw a couple wild cats heading in Casper's direction. I cautioned Willie. He looked over at the cats and began flickering around Casper. He tried to nudge Casper to direct him home.

No such luck.

Three loud cat meows came from my cat watch—fifteen minutes to go.

Casper kept pacing toward the feral cats with his tail straight up in the air. The cats approached and circled around him. One of them, most likely the leader, stepped forward from the pack. Casper and the leader positioned themselves in a low, snarling attack position. They began to hiss and meow. It was an eerie sound, like babies crying.

Willie grew upset. He fluttered above Casper, but there was nothing he could do.

More alarms meowed from my cat watch—ten minutes to go.

At that moment, a catfight broke out. Casper and the wild cat jumped on top of each other and began rolling around. Loud meows were followed by hissing, pawing, and scratching. The noise was dreadful. Out of instinct, Willie and I leaped on top of each cat—he landed on Casper while I tried to separate the wild cat from Casper. We desperately tried to stop the fight. Instead, Willie and I got tangled up in the fight, rolling around with the two of them.

The awful sounds were followed by more hissing, scratching, and rolling around. There was nothing Willie and I could do to stop the fight!

A final meow came from my cat watch—five minutes left. "Willie, Willie!" I shouted. "We have to go! We can't stay—otherwise we won't be able to help Casper."

Willie didn't listen. He kept forcing himself between the two cats. Finally I grabbed Willie by the neck and pried him away. "We have to go now!"

The two of us shouted, *"Brastic, astik!"* Off we flew through the city of Seattle, into the Earth's sky, into the fresh ozone layer of the Heavenly World, and back to our angel clouds. The entire flight home, I kept hearing the hissing and meowing of the catfight. As soon as we landed, we chanted the magic code. Our wings disappeared from our backs and landed in front of the four guide helpers. They flew off into the distance carrying our beautiful glowing wings.

I was still shaking when they left. Willie was completely dismayed. He was rolling around on his angel cloud, still trying to stop the catfight. After a few minutes, we settled down.

"That didn't go too well, did it, Minka?" Willie said.

"No, it didn't." I was distraught about the fight. Years ago I'd seen a mean and lean catfight between Muris and a neighborhood cat—but this one was dreadful. I could still hear the loud, piercing meows. I had no idea what to do to help Casper.

"Let's get a good night's sleep and think of a plan tomorrow," I told Willie. Then I put my head between my paws to try and make the meowing noise go away.

Willie didn't answer. For the rest of the night he sat on top of his angel cloud, thinking about Casper.

13. Casper's Victory

The next morning, Willie and I woke before Chloe and Oscar appeared on our angel clouds. We patiently waited, hoping they would be able to give us an idea about what to do for Casper.

When they finally arrived, they went about their morning ritual. Breakfast was followed by an oil and soap bath. They made no reference to our Earthly trip.

"Chloe, I'm not sure what to do about Casper," I said finally.

"The two of you will need to figure that out," Chloe answered impassively. She rinsed the oil and soap from my fur. "The fight went on for a few more minutes after you left. Casper fared well, with only a few scratches on his nose. The wild cat was more hurt, but not enough to stop him from getting into another fight with Casper in the future."

"Will we see another fight on our next trip to Earth?" I asked.

"I'm not sure what will happen—everything constantly changes on Earth," Chloe told me. "Up here, we only see things as they happen. It's up to you and Willie to decide what to do."

I felt dismayed. Chloe had given us no direction about our next trip.

For the rest of the afternoon I lay next to Willie on his angel cloud. We needed strength from each other to regain our angel powers before returning to Earth.

"We have to stop the next fight," I told Willie. "We need a way to stop those wild cats from coming after Casper."

When midnight came, Willie and I were still exhausted from our last trip. As soon as Chloe, Oscar, and the guide helpers appeared, with little enthusiasm, Willie and I said, *"Sastik, mastic, kulik, pelik, skeber, veber, milip, tips."* Our heavenly wings appeared on our backs.

We ran forward, and with a sluggish *"Brastic, astik!"* we fluttered into the air.

Our angel wings quickly whooshed us to the left, and we descended through the ozone layer of the Heavenly World and into the Earth's sphere. The flight was very turbulent as we traveled through heavy, dark clouds before we descended into Seattle. I was worried whether this was an ominous sign of our visit with Casper. We soon arrived at Willie's Earth home.

Willie and I browsed around, not expecting to find Casper. Suddenly, Willie nudged me. Casper was sleeping on one of the cat posts.

"What should we do?" Willie asked as he fluttered toward Casper.

"Wait for Casper to make a move."

We waited and waited, hoping Casper would give us a sign. I had to force myself not to fall asleep.

Finally, we sensed movement. Casper yawned, stretched, and licked his paws—then repositioned himself and drifted off into another catnap. To my dismay, I saw that time was quickly ticking away. I was anxious. To calm myself I decided to leap from one end of the room to the other and do a few somersault moves. Willie was a bit dismayed at my behavior.

"Minka, stay focused!" exclaimed Willie.

"Oh, all right," I answered as I moved next to Willie.

After almost two hours, Casper woke. With a soft grunting noise, he stretched. He jumped off the cat post as soon as he heard Anna leave the kitchen and go down the stairs to the front door. Casper ran toward the door. He waited until Anna opened the door and then quickly ran outdoors. Willie and I fluttered along behind. It was raining. Casper ran up the street and immediately made a right turn. We watched Casper wander from one bush to another and then dart into a neighbor's yard.

Willie and I pointed our ears to the left and followed him. Casper searched around a few bushes before running to the next yard.

"Wow, Willie. I'm not surprised you felt Casper needed help," I meowed. "He's definitely looking for trouble."

"Maybe even looking for the wild cats," Willie answered.

"What kind of cat would look for a fight?" I asked. "Plus, it's too wet to be outdoors."

"It's the Siamese in him. I don't believe Casper actually searches for a fight, but he does have an unsettled nature and needs a challenge. Maybe these wild cats bothered him at some point, and now he's trying to regain his territory and respect."

We kept following Casper. Finally, when he reached a cul-de-sac, Casper found what he was looking for—the pack of wild cats. They were rummaging through some garbage, hunting for food. Casper trotted over and sat in a perfect upright position, his tail lashing back and forth. He began to meow loudly.

The leader answered Casper with a dreadful meow. The other wild cats immediately lifted their backs in fearsome half-moon shapes. They ran over to Casper and made a circle around him.

Willie flew above Casper. My stomach was in knots. I was not a combative cat, and had lived on Earth without ever fighting with another cat. Yet I could feel a rush going through my body and felt myself shifting into fight mode.

I edged nearer to the circle as I tried to figure out which cat I was going to fight.

Casper moved slowly toward the leader. The leader stood his ground and meowed piercingly several times. Casper took on a fight stance, low to the wet ground. Willie moved slightly ahead of Casper and positioned himself close to the ground as well. I focused intently on the wild cat leader.

As soon as he lunged forward to attack Casper, I intercepted him and knocked him to the ground. The leader sneezed, slid, rolled over, and then stood up. He was shaken from falling to the ground without Casper touching him. The leader took one step closer to Casper, and then another. Casper moved slightly toward the leader while Willie moved in front of Casper.

Casper leaped forward, sneezed, and pounced on the leader. With the exact same move, Willie landed on the leader's back. The three rolled around, sliding in the wet rain, gnawing and scratching. Finally Willie grabbed the leader by the neck and pinned him to the ground.

The loud cat meows came from my cat watch—there were fifteen minutes left.

Silence followed the fight. Then the leader stood up, shook his head, and arched his body into a half-moon shape. Another piercing meow followed.

Casper stayed down, his ears back and his tail lashing like a whip. He loudly returned the meow, as if a greater force was plotting this fight.

Before the leader could make a move, I flew to him, grabbed him by the neck, and lifted him high into the air. Holding on to the leader's neck with my teeth, I flicked my tail and made two perfect circles. Then I pointed my paws down and deposited the leader cat on the other side of the street.

When Casper saw the wild cat fly over him and twirl in the air, his fur stood up and his tail fluttered. The leader seemed very perplexed as to how he had ended up on the other side of the street. His buddies were alarmed too. They ran and slunk behind the garbage cans.

More meows from my cat watch—ten minutes to go.

The rain was pouring down. I could hear thunder in the distance. Despite the eeriness of the fight, the leader didn't hesitate to make a run at Casper. Again, I intercepted him. He sneezed as I grabbed him by the neck and fluttered him over to the garbage cans near his buddies.

This time the leader regained his wits and jumped forward with all his force to try and land on Casper. Willie was instantly on the leader's back, pulling him away. Instead of fighting with Casper, the leader tried to paw at Willie.

Casper quickly leaped to the other side of the street and watched the leader roll around on the wet ground while pawing at the air. Willie would not let go. He pulled the leader into a ditch before finally releasing him and flying over to me.

This time the leader had enough. As soon as he was able to get out of the ditch, he ran over to his buddies, and the whole pack disappeared in the wink of a cat's eye. Casper stayed close to the ground. He seemed uncertain as to whether the wild cats would return.

Meanwhile, my cat watch indicated we had only five minutes left.

"We did it!" shouted Willie.

"We did, and we have to go," I told him.

During the trip back to Cat Heaven, I felt unsettled. We had fended off the wild cat leader, but I wasn't sure just how or if we had helped Casper. The guide helpers greeted us at our angel clouds. We chanted our code and the wings disappeared from our backs. Off they went, carrying our glowing wings.

Willie seemed elated but exhausted. "I'm sure Casper won't fight again!" he shouted.

I didn't want to say anything, but that was my fear exactly.

14. A Lesson Learned

Early the next morning Willie was still talking about the fight. "We sure scared those wild cats away!" he shouted. "Casper may not have to fight again. Now he can stay indoors without our help."

When Chloe and Oscar appeared at our angel clouds, the answer was clear.

"That is not quite right," Chloe said sternly. "In fact, the opposite is true. Your efforts to pull the cat leader away from Casper have made him feel invincible. Now he feels he can win any fight. He's roaming the neighborhood more than he ever did before!"

"Uh oh," Willie said. He looked deflated.

Oscar fluttered over to Willie and began licking his ears to soothe him.

Chloe gazed at me sternly. "Unfortunately, since Casper's fight, he's had two more fights, one with another cat in his neighborhood and the other with a coyote after dark. Casper was slightly injured during the first fight and barely escaped the coyote. It seems he was convinced all he needed to do was whoosh his tail back and forth and the other cat or animal would go flying."

Willie and I hung our heads, and Willie kneaded his angel cloud. The gut feeling I had had after our second visit to Casper was right. What we did for Casper hadn't kept him from straying from his home.

"I know you guys meant well," interjected Oscar, "but you may have done Casper more harm than good."

Willie curled into a small ball and didn't move, even while Oscar fussed all over him.

Chloe turned to me. "Minka, I'm not sure you even had a plan for Casper. And you've only got one more trip to help him."

Willie twitched his ears. He'd heard what Chloe had said.

"Rest and think. We'll be back at midnight," Chloe added. She and Oscar fluttered away. I stayed on my angel cloud and thought about what to do. Finally I fell into a long catnap. When I awoke, Willie was pacing around his angel cloud.

I could tell he had not taken a nap. He was in deep thought. I had never seen this side of Willie before. I watched as he moved from one end of his cloud, peered down to catch a glimpse of Earth, twitched his tail, moved to the other end of cloud, and then repeated it all again.

Suddenly he stopped. "I got it!" Willie shouted. "I have the plan!"

He pounced over to my angel cloud and began whispering in my ear. I chuckled. He went on and on.

I laughed and rolled onto my back with my legs straight up in the air. "That's funny, but it's still an awesome plan. I think it might even work!"

Willie began dashing around in excitement.

"Hey, calm down!" I warned him. "We'll need all our angel powers if your plan is going to be a success."

When midnight arrived, we were waiting when Chloe, Oscar, and the guide helpers appeared on our angel clouds.

"My, you two look refreshed," remarked Chloe.

"Are you geared up for your last trip to visit Casper?" asked Oscar.

"Yep, ready to go!" Willie meowed. "It's my plan and we're ready to execute it!"

Together we shouted, *"Sastik, mastic, kulik, pelik, skeber, veber, milip, tips!"* Instantly our heavenly wings appeared on our backs. We both ran forward and shouted, *"Brastic, astik!"* and fluttered into the air.

Quickly we descended through the fresh, clean ozone layer of the Heavenly World and into the Earth's sphere. We traveled for miles to the city of Seattle. Finally we arrived at Willie's home.

Willie didn't waste any time finding Casper. He was lounging on his cat post in the living room. Willie ran over and nudged his face. Casper sneezed, curled up into a small ball, and fell asleep.

Willie flew to the kitchen and began pawing at one of the cupboards in search of catnip. This would be the incentive to get Casper moving.

"I'll get the cupboard door open," I meowed. "You need to save your angel power for the rest of the plan."

Once I clawed the door open, Willie snatched the bag of catnip in his mouth and darted into the living room. He tore the bag open and sprinkled catnip near Casper's cat post. He then fluttered over Casper and gnawed at his neck. Casper awoke, sneezed, and smelled the catnip.

Immediately he jumped toward the cat post and rolled around in the catnip. Casper darted from one end of the living room to the other, rolled around some more, and kneaded the carpet. He took another hit of the catnip, and then ran over to the front door as he heard Anna unlocking it. He was out the door the instant it opened. Willie and I quickly followed him.

Outside, Casper hesitated. He looked toward the street, but instead of running away, he began to roam around in the garden. He pawed at the grass, wandered near some bushes, sniffed a few flowerpots, and then settled in the grass.

"Maybe he's scared to leave home because of his last fight," I whispered. "He doesn't want to get hurt. Perhaps he's already learned his lesson."

Willie didn't seem convinced. "No, I know Casper. His eyes tell me everything. Casper may act cautious for a day or two, but he will go back to roaming the streets," Willie said as he twitched his tail back and forth. "We need to complete our plan to make sure Casper's wandering days are over."

In a flash, Willie grabbed Casper by his neck and fluttered up the street. Pointing his ear left, he flew Casper over to a neighbor's front yard and dropped him onto the grass. Casper seemed startled and unsure of how he had ended up in another yard.

Willie then went in search of the neighbor's cat, whom Casper had fought.

"Do you need me to do anything?" I asked.

"Get the golden dust ready," Willie answered as he fluttered around looking for the other cat. I reached for my collar, tugged at the sack to open it, and placed a pinch of golden dust in my right paw.

Willie found the neighbor cat in the backyard sniffing at a flowerpot. He grabbed the cat by his neck and carried him to the front yard. As soon as Casper saw him, he hissed and positioned himself in a low sideways crouch.

The two cats seemed distressed, unsure of what was happening. Nevertheless, by instinct, they faced one another and began to meow loudly. Casper's back arched in a half-moon shape. The neighborhood cat leaped up and landed a few feet in front of Casper.

Just before Casper was about to attack, Willie shouted to me, "Make the wish and throw the golden dust at the neighbor cat!"

I shook my right paw and sprinkled the cat with golden dust. Then I made my wish.

Instantly, the cat became three times his size, almost as big as a tiger! His meow was now a terrifying roar. Casper froze in terror.

"Oh, boy, this sure is great!" I exclaimed as I rolled over in the grass.

Using all his angel powers, Willie took the large cat by the neck and lifted him high into the air. Tightly curling his body, he did two somersaults and then dropped the cat back down in front of Casper. Again, the large cat roared.

Casper darted into the bushes and, in a wink, high-tailed it down the street toward home.

The large cat's roar was so startling that I, too, ran into the bushes.

"It's okay, Minka, the large cat is gone. Come out of the bushes," chuckled Willie. "It was only the golden dust that made the cat so large."

"I got caught up in the moment," I replied as I staggered out of the bushes and pawed a few leaves off my fur.

The loud cat meows sounded from my cat watch—fifteen minutes left.

Inside the house, Casper was hiding behind his cat post. Trembling, he focused on the beautiful translucent glow that seemed to come from the living room. It made him feel safe, as safe as he could be. All that he needed was right here.

Staring at the golden sparkles shimmering in the air, Casper slowly moved out from behind the cat post. Then he saw Willie and me standing in front of him. Our wings glistened with their radiant colors.

"Willie, is that you?" Casper exclaimed. "Are you really here?"

"Yes, Casper, it is me," Willie answered as his wings flickered.

"You were so sick the last time I saw you. I tried to help you get better, but . . ." Casper put his head down sadly. "You were taken away and I never saw you again."

"Remember the day I went outdoors?" Willie asked.

When Casper nodded, Willie continued. "I got stuck outside in the cold all night long. It was raining, and I got real hungry and cold. I might have eaten something that wasn't good for me, or maybe it was the dampness—but when I went back into the house the next morning, I couldn't stop shivering and sneezing."

"I tried to get you back indoors," meowed Casper. "I scratched at the door, but the door would not open. Anna did not want me to run outdoors too. She was so worried about you. She kept calling for you from her bedroom window."

"It's all right," Willie told him. "I am in a very good place. Remember Minka?" he added.

"I sure do! The two of you look like angels and have bright and colorful wings," Casper answered.

"We are angels," Willie told him as he opened his wings wide. "Minka and I have come from Cat Heaven to help you learn to stay at home and not wander outdoors, where you might be in danger or get sick. I don't want the same thing to happen to you that happened to me."

The loud cat meows sounded from my cat watch—ten minutes to go.

Casper looked curious. "Cat Heaven—is there really such a place?"

"Yes, it's where we go after we spend our time on Earth," Willie explained. "We can watch over our cat friends from Cat Heaven."

"Will I go there, too?" asked Casper.

"Yes, when your time comes to join us," Willie said softly. "But you have to promise not to roam outdoors and get into fights."

"I learned my lesson," answered Casper. "For you, Willie, I will promise anything."

Willie nudged Casper with his head and licked his ears. "I can feel you, Willie," Casper stated as he slowly looked into Willie's eyes.

"You will always feel me near you. I am right beside you, whatever you do and wherever you go."

"I miss you, Willie," Casper meowed softly. "But I know I will be safe, with you guiding my days."

The cat meows sounded from my cat watch—five minutes left.

"We have to go," Willie meowed as he nudged Casper's forehead one last time and gazed into his eyes. "Remember this vision of me, and all will be well with you."

Willie and I positioned ourselves in front of Casper. Our wings, made up of thousands of shimmering bird feathers, opened wide.

As Casper stared in amazement, for a moment he, too, took on an angelic appearance.

"Until we meet again," Willie whispered.

Then the two of us shouted, *"Brastic, astik!"* Off we flew through the city of Seattle. Willie was elated and humming a cat tune as we made our way through the Earth's sky, into the fresh ozone layer of Heavenly World, and back to our angel clouds.

Willie insisted on keeping his angel wings on his back for a brief moment after we landed. He told the guide helpers that he wanted to savor the moment for a bit longer. The guide helpers nervously looked at one another, not sure if the protocol could be changed. They shrugged their shoulders and looked off into the distance, and then looked back at Willie and nodded in unison. Willie fluttered around on his angel cloud, reenacting the scene when Casper saw him in his angel form.

"Okay, time's up," stated one of the guide helpers.

We chanted our magic code and our wings disappeared from our backs. The guide helpers flew off into the distance, making their loud *rat-ta-ta* flapping sound and carrying our beautiful, glowing wings.

That night Willie and I fell asleep as soon as our heads hit our angel pillows.

15. Sofia

Oscar appeared at Willie's angel cloud midmorning. He arranged for the guide helpers to set up a lavish buffet of all sorts of cat food on Willie's angel cloud. Oscar was helping get the buffet ready when Willie finally yawned and stretched awake.

"Good morning, my hero!" shouted Oscar. "I have an excellent assortment of food for you to select from for your breakfast."

Willie sat up and smiled.

"Go on, choose your meal. You used up a lot of angel powers, and I want to make sure you get your strength back," Oscar urged Willie as he fluttered around and tucked a napkin in his collar.

Willie was famished. He chose all his favorite cat food brands and settled down for his morning meal. Oscar made sure he had enough water to drink and a second helping of his favorite food.

"Minka," Oscar shouted over to my angel cloud, "there is plenty for you too. Come, come and eat!"

I yawned and stretched, licked my paws, and leaped over to Willie's cloud. "Where's Chloe?" I asked as I filled my plate.

"She'll be here shortly," answered Oscar. "She had to meet with the Angel Leaders about your progress with your Earthly wish. Don't worry," he added, "the Angel Leaders are very impressed with what you both have done for Muris and Casper."

I looked at Willie and smiled.

"Casper already has a new playmate," Oscar meowed. "Her name is Lulu. At first Casper was a bit frightened because she has the coloring of a tiger. Casper didn't go near her, thinking she might grow to become three times her size. After some time passed, he realized she was a new friend and not someone who would fight him. Now Casper fusses over Lulu and they have become real pals. He is happy staying inside and playing with Lulu."

"That's great!" shouted Willie. He finished eating and began to lick his paws.

"You two have done a remarkable job," Chloe announced as she appeared on my angel cloud. "I must admit, I was unsure that you could help Casper, but I was amazed by Willie's plan and his determination in making it happen, and how well you worked together to save Casper. The Angel Leaders are very enthusiastic about the progress you have made so far."

The guide helpers cleared our breakfast away. Chloe and Oscar began their ritual of bathing us. They lathered us with a lot of oils and soap. Then the soap was rinsed from our fur.

"Oscar and I will let you rest for a day, but we will return tomorrow at midnight," Chloe told me as she twitched her tail back and forth. "One word of caution—even though you have done a great job with Muris and Casper, you still have two cats left to help to complete your Earthly wish."

After spending so much time with Chloe in Cat Heaven, I knew this was her way of telling me not to get overconfident. We nodded. Our angel buddies fluttered above our angel clouds and flew into the horizon.

Then I turned to face Willie. "Our next visits are to Sofia," I said. Both of us knew her very well. She had lived with Casper and Willie for years, and then with Muris and me.

"When Sofia lived with us, she was queen of the house and ate all the food. She became big and fat," explained Willie. "Then, when she moved to your house, Muris wouldn't let her eat all the food and she lost weight."

"That's right," I said. "Sometimes Sofia has too much sugar in her body. It's called diabetes. She needs medicine and a really good diet to control her blood sugar. Otherwise she could get really sick, or even die."

Willie looked solemn. "We have to help her understand she must eat healthy cat food as well as exercise."

We slept the whole day and into the morning of the next day. We relaxed on our angel clouds until midnight arrived. After our trips to help Muris and Casper, we knew not to count too much on what would happen during our first visit to Sofia. We would first need to assess the situation before moving forward.

Chloe, Oscar, and the guide helpers appeared at our angel clouds. I gazed up at the sky and then looked over at Willie, who was standing in his preflight position: front legs slightly bent, head and chest forward, ready to go.

Together Willie and I shouted, *"Sastik, mastic, kulik, pelik, skeber, veber, milip, tips!"* Our heavenly wings appeared on our backs.

"Brastic, astik!" we stated, and fluttered up into the air. Our

angel wings quickly whooshed us to the left, and then, as fast as the speed of light, we descended through the ozone layer of the Heavenly World and into the Earth's sphere.

The sky was getting lighter. Again, our angel wings whooshed us to the left and downward through fluffy gray clouds. It was raining as we approached Seattle. I had a hard time seeing the beautiful landmarks of the city. We traveled north along the interstate and kept descending. Finally, we reached my old home.

We landed inside my bedroom, fluttered to the bedroom door, and peered down the hallway. No cat or dog in sight. We fluttered to the living room, where we found Muris next to Lana. They were fast asleep. Every so often Lana would quiver her eyes slightly open and then grunt and fall back asleep. She was having one of her happy dog dreams. Muris would twitch his ears whenever Lana grunted, then reposition himself closer to her. The scene was heartwarming.

Willie and I found Sofia sleeping next to the sliding glass door in the dining room. I looked out at the deck and thought about how Willie and I had taught Muris his lesson not that long ago. I smiled, knowing that Muris had become a changed cat.

I gazed down at Sofia. She was still as beautiful as ever. Her fur was brown and gray with symmetrical black stripes along her back. Her tummy and paws were pure white, and her tail was marked with gray and black stripes. Sofia had a very dear tiger face with gentle green eyes. Her nose was shaped just like a tiger's. She had such a soft, pleasant meow.

Then I noticed that Sofia had lost weight. I wasn't too concerned, since I figured she must be playing with Muris and getting the exercise she needed.

"What should we do now?" asked Willie.

"We should assess the situation before thinking up a plan to help Sofia," I answered. "We're not sure what help she needs. If she is eating well, then we need to assist her in exercising more. She has lost a little bit of weight since our visits to help Muris. Maybe she is exercising too much and we need to get her to eat on a more regular basis. Let's just watch her for a while."

Willie and I sat down next to Sofia. She didn't budge an inch. After some time, Willie became restless. He decided to do a few somersaults in the air and then fly through the different rooms of the house. I, too, decided to do a few summersault moves in the living room. Then I lay down next to Sofia while Muris slept contently next to Lana.

When Willie returned, he asked about the medicine Sofia needed. "What should we do about that?"

"I remember Sofia needed the medicine twice a day," I stated. "I think it was called insulin. I don't think we have to worry about giving it to her."

"What happens if she doesn't get her medicine?" Willie asked as he licked his right front paw and straightened out his back angel wing feathers.

"That's a good question, but I don't know the answer. Let's just focus on her food."

Just then, Sofia got up. She moved unhurriedly to the bedroom. Willie and I twitched our ears to the left and followed behind. I was alarmed at how slowly she walked. She seemed extremely tired.

"I always thought Sofia had a little more spunk," commented Willie.

"She did," I meowed worriedly.

"Maybe she had a big playdate with Muris and it drained her energy," Willie responded. "Look at Muris sleeping next to Lana.

He seems pooped too!"

Willie's observation made a lot of sense. I tried not to worry as we followed Sofia. She took her time sniffing the ground and then stopping to lick her fur before slowly resuming her amble.

Sofia meowed as if she needed something and then went into the bedroom. Willie and I flew above her and watched as Sofia located her food dish near the entrance to the bathroom. She sniffed at the food and then plopped down near her dish.

The loud cat meows sounded from my cat watch—fifteen minutes left.

By now I was very worried. Sofia seemed sluggish and her eyes had lost their soft glow.

"Push the food dish over to her," I meowed to Willie.

Willie concentrated and managed to move the dish. Sofia didn't seem to notice the dish moving. She showed no interest in the food, even though it was right in front of her. I fluttered around and tried to nudge her a bit so she would get a scent of the food.

The loud cat meows sounded from my cat watch—ten minutes to go.

I concentrated, grabbed a bit of food from her dish, and placed the food on her front paw. Again, she didn't flinch.

"Oh, dear, something is wrong." My tail lashed back and forth and my angel wings spread wide open.

Willie and I began to whisper in Sofia's ear, telling her to eat the food. She didn't even sneeze.

The cat meows sounded from my cat watch—five minutes left.

"We have to go, Minka," Willie said, nudging my back.

"I know, but something is terribly wrong with Sofia," I

meowed as tears filled my eyes.

Reluctantly I tore myself away from Sofia. The two of us shouted, *"Brastic, astik!"* On the entire trip back to Cat Heaven, I could think only of Sofia.

The guide helpers were waiting as we arrived. We chanted our code and our wings disappeared from our backs and landed in front of the four guide helpers. The guide helpers flew off into the distance carrying our beautiful, glowing wings.

Willie fell asleep as soon as his head hit his angel pillow, but I was awake almost the entire night, thinking of dear, beautiful Sofia. What could we possibly do? Could we help her, or was it already too late?

16. A Call for Help

I was anxious the next day, thinking about Sofia. I couldn't wait to get back to Earth. Willie tried to distract me with funny stories about what the other cats were doing on different angel clouds. "Look, Minka, see that calico cat on the angel cloud in the far left corner from our clouds? He's heading over to introduce himself to that beautiful white cat who just arrived in Cat Heaven."

I looked over and saw the calico cat about to make his move. Then one of the guide helpers grabbed him by the neck and flew him back to his angel cloud. It was very funny and I almost laughed—until my thoughts returned to Sofia.

When midnight came, Chloe and Oscar fluttered over to our angel clouds. The guide helpers were making their loud *rat-ta-ta* flapping sound. Carrying our beautiful glowing wings, they followed closely behind.

Willie and I quickly shouted, *"Sastik, mastic, kulik, pelik, skeber, veber, milip, tips!*" Our heavenly wings instantly appeared on our backs.

Without hesitation, we both ran forward and shouted, "*Brastic, astik!*" and fluttered up into the air.

With a flash of light, we descended through the Heavenly World, to the city of Seattle, and to my Earth home, where we landed inside my old bedroom.

I looked around the bedroom and then at the entrance to the bathroom. Sofia was lying next to her food dish. I flew over to her, and Willie followed. When I nudged her, she didn't move.

Now I was really alarmed. Placing my head on her chest, I could feel her chest move slightly. "Willie, Sofia is very, very sick!" I meowed as I fluttered over her. I nudged her side, pushed her front paws, and bit her neck and tail, but Sofia didn't respond.

Willie also checked Sofia, making sure not to get in my way. He licked her head and ears. He looked as frightened as I felt.

"Willie, I don't know what to do!" I meowed loudly.

Willie lifted his right paw and pointed.

"What is it?" I looked at him. "What are you pointing at?"

"Your iPhone," he whispered.

I suddenly remembered the special Heavenly iPhone dangling from my cat collar. I tore the iPhone from my collar with trembling paws, dialed Cat Heaven, and waited for someone to answer our call for help.

"This is Chloe speaking," said the voice on the other end of the line.

"Chloe, we have an emergency!" I shouted. "Sofia is really sick and we don't know what to do for her!"

"Minka, listen to me carefully," Chloe said firmly. "You will

need to give Sofia her insulin."

"Her what?"

"The medicine," answered Chloe.

"Oh yes, that's right, insulin," I said breathlessly. "But how?"

"The insulin is stored in the refrigerator in the kitchen. I need you to open the refrigerator door and get the medicine and a syringe," Chloe instructed.

Willie and I twitched our ears to the left and fluttered into the kitchen. Willie began pawing at the refrigerator door, but he couldn't get the door open.

When I reported the problem to Chloe, there was a pause. "You will need to use your golden dust to open the door," she said finally.

"No, no, we mustn't use the dust—we might need it for our final visit!" I cried.

"If you don't use it now, there may not be a last visit with Sofia," Chloe reminded me. "This task will take only a very small portion."

I trembled as I reached for the golden dust around my collar. I tugged the sack open and placed a scant portion of the golden dust in my right paw. Then I sprinkled the refrigerator door with the golden dust and made my wish.

Instantly, the refrigerator opened. "It worked," I told Chloe.

"The insulin is on the top shelf by the butter dish," Chloe told me. "It is in a small glass vial, and it looks like water. Do you see it?"

Willie hovered near the top shelf of the refrigerator. He used his angel power to move a few of the food items until he spotted the butter dish. Next to it was a little bottle of clear liquid. Willie snatched it in his right paw.

126

"We have the insulin!" I meowed into the iPhone.

"Good work. Next, find the box of syringes in the cupboard drawer next to the refrigerator," stated Chloe. "You will need to use a pinch of golden dust to open the drawer."

I didn't give her an argument this time. I placed a tiny portion of golden dust in my paw and sprinkled it over the cupboard drawer. As soon as I found the box of syringes, I pawed the box open and grabbed one of them. Luckily, the sharp end of the needle was covered with an orange safety cap.

"We have the syringe," I told Chloe.

"Great work—now get back to Sofia," Chloe instructed.

We flew back into the bedroom and landed next to Sofia. She was still not moving. I placed my head on her chest and could feel her chest slightly rise.

"We are at Sofia's side," I spoke into the iPhone.

"This next part will be a bit tricky. I need both of you to remain very calm while I explain how much insulin to put in the syringe," Chloe said. "We want to be sure to give Sofia just enough insulin to keep her alive until she can get to the hospital."

"The syringe is marked with ten black lines. Do you see the lines?" asked Chloe.

I held the syringe upright in my paws, and Willie and I inspected it. "I think Chloe means these lines," stated Willie as he pawed the syringe to show me the black marks.

"Yes, we see the black lines," I said into the iPhone.

"Minka, I want you to place the small glass vial between your paws," responded Chloe. "I want Willie to place the syringe in his paws and push the syringe into the rubbery top portion of the glass vial. Willie will need to pull back on the syringe's plunger very carefully with his mouth, only to the second black line," stated Chloe.

I handed Willie the syringe.

Slowly he moved the needle into the top of the vial. When he started to move the needle into the vial, there was a bit of resistance. He dropped the needle from his paws. "I'm not sure I can do this," meowed Willie.

"Just concentrate on how we must help Sofia and move the syringe slowly into the vial," I reassured him. I held the vial between my paws as Willie repositioned the syringe and cautiously pushed the needle into the vial. Ever so slowly, he pulled back on the syringe plunger with his mouth until the insulin reached the right line. Then he pulled the syringe back from the vial with his paws.

"We did it!" I told Chloe. Just then, loud cat meows sounded from my cat watch—fifteen minutes to go.

"Minka, stay calm," Chloe reminded me. "The two of you need to give Sofia her medicine. Willie needs to clutch Sofia's neck and lift her fur, just like the guide helpers lifted you up to bring you to the Angel Castle," Chloe explained. "Minka, you place the syringe in your paws. In the soft part of Sofia's neck, push it past her fur and into her skin."

The loud cat meows sounded from my cat watch—ten minutes left.

I looked down at Sofia. There was no time to waste. I nodded at Willie, who clutched Sofia's neck and lifted her fur just as Chloe had instructed. I held the syringe in my paws and pushed the sharp end into her fur and through her skin. I didn't feel any resistance. With my mouth I pushed the insulin into the open space.

Done! For safety's sake, I rolled the exposed needle into

the furnace vent in the floor. Then the two of us collapsed beside Sofia.

Within a minute, Sofia's front paws began to move. She softly meowed and moved her head. I placed my head between her front paws and her head. She sneezed and softly meowed again.

I licked her forehead and whispered into her ears, "You're going to be all right." I made sure to leave the sealed bottle of insulin near her food dish, where Valerie would see it and make sure she got to the animal hospital.

The loud cat meows sounded from my cat watch. "Time to go," I heard Chloe say.

With that, I turned off the iPhone and refastened it to my collar. Willie and I slowly drew away from Sofia.

The two of us shouted, *"Brastic, astik!"* Our angel wings spread open, and off we flew through the city of Seattle, into the Earth's sky and the fresh ozone layer of the Heavenly World, and back home to Cat Heaven.

When we arrived at our angel clouds, the guide helpers, Chloe, and Oscar were waiting for us. We chanted our code and our wings disappeared from our backs. The guide helpers flew off, carrying our beautiful, glowing wings. Oscar soothed Willie to sleep. Chloe positioned herself next to me until I fell asleep. They both left our angel clouds while we were deep in our dreams.

17. All Ends Well

I felt Chloe's right paw on my back as she leaned over to lick my ears. "Sofia is going to be all right," she whispered.

I rolled over and stretched, and then sat upright to face Chloe.

"Willie and you did a remarkable job of saving Sofia's life," she said. "She isn't completely out of trouble, but she's being well cared for at the hospital."

I peered into Chloe's eyes while she updated me on Sofia's condition. "Sofia hadn't been eating for several days before you arrived on your first trip to visit her. Since she wasn't feeling well, she would hide underneath the bed and may not have received her medicine," Chloe explained as she kneaded my back. "She was in a bad diabetic condition when you came for your second visit. She likely would have died if you and Willie hadn't been there to save her."

"What can we do for her now?" I asked.

"Oh, you still have plenty of work to do," replied Chloe. "You have to help her understand how important it is to eat a balanced diet and get her medicine on a regular basis."

I was surprised that Chloe was giving me so much information. She hadn't provided many clues about what to do for Muris and Casper. Maybe knowing we had worked so hard to save Sofia's life made her feel that we deserved some Heavenly insight.

"We don't have much golden dust left," I said, worried.

"Golden dust isn't always the answer," she replied. "You may have to use your angel wisdom to help her instead."

"But Sofia won't be able to see us without the golden dust," I protested.

"Wait and see. You have a lot of angel powers, if you learn to rely on them," replied Chloe. "Remember, in Cat Heaven we don't know what will happen during your next trip, since everything changes instantly on Earth. We can only see things as they happen. It is up to the two of you to know what to do on Earth to help your friends. It's all part of your Earthly wish."

As Chloe bathed me, Oscar fluttered over to Willie's angel cloud to wake him up and begin bathing him as well. Even though this was a change in sequence of morning events, Willie enjoyed being pampered before his breakfast arrived. After the bath ritual, Willie and I ate in silence. We fell asleep as soon as the dishes were cleared from our angel clouds.

I finally awoke from my long catnap in the late afternoon. I saw Willie stretch and paw at his angel cloud. "Minka, we really helped Sofia, didn't we?" he called to me.

"We saved her life," I responded with a wink.

"So what do we do for her during our last trip?"

"Chloe hinted that we need to spend time just talking to her," I told Willie. "But I'm not sure how we can do that without our golden dust. Let's nap some more and not think about it too much."

"Sounds like the perfect plan," Willie declared as he curled up into a ball on his angel cloud.

"Even though we need some sort of plan to help our friends, we also need to wait and see what will happen on Earth when we arrive," I meowed to Willie as I dozed off for another nap.

Before I knew it, it was time for our last visit to Sofia. I heard the guide helpers making their loud *rat-ta-ta* flapping sound as they headed toward us, carrying our beautiful, glowing wings. Chloe and Oscar instantly appeared at our angel clouds.

Willie and I were still groggy from our long naps. We slowly positioned ourselves in our flight stance. *"Sastik, mastic, kulik, pelik, skeber, veber, milip, tips!"* Our heavenly wings instantly appeared on our backs.

"Brastic, astik!" and the two of us fluttered into the air.

Our angel wings quickly whooshed us to the left, and we descended through the fresh, clean ozone layer of the Heavenly World into the Earth's sphere and to the city of Seattle.

Suddenly I noticed our wings were moving us in a different direction than my Earthly home. We traveled along the interstate until we crossed a big lake and then headed slightly east into an urban neighborhood full of buildings. We landed inside a large room in one of the buildings.

All sorts of cats and dogs were lying on stretchers. Most of the animals were quiet, except for a few who were whimpering softly. Some of the animals had tubes tied to their front legs, and the tubes were connected to a clear sack of liquid positioned above their heads. Others had big screens above their heads that made strange beeping sounds while colorful marks darted across them.

Willie looked startled. "Where are we, Minka?" he asked as his tail lashed back and forth.

"I'm not sure," I meowed back.

"Do you think the dogs will see us and begin to bark?" he asked nervously.

"No, I don't think they can see us," I reassured him.

We started to tiptoe across the big room and peer at each of the animals. Willie fluttered above the animals and sighed.

"They look like they are sick or hurt," he commented sadly.

"That's it!" I shouted. "We are at the animal hospital! Sofia should be here somewhere!"

Willie didn't hesitate. He began flying around to find Sofia. "She's over here, Minka!" he exclaimed a few minutes later.

I flew to the left corner of the room to find Sofia nestled in some warm blankets. She looked very peaceful. With our angel wings wide open, we positioned ourselves beside her. Willie purred close to her right side. I was on her left side nudging her paw.

Both of us concentrated on Sofia's well-being. As our angel wings softly fluttered, a beautiful translucent mist flickered from them. I had never seen our wings do this before. I stared in awe as the angelic haze from our wings formed a cloud and shimmered over Sofia, touching her ever so lightly.

Slowly Sofia's eyes opened. They flickered a bit and then focused directly on me. "Minka, is that you?" she whispered.

"Yes, it is," I responded.

Sofia looked at me and then turned her head to look at Willie, who was still purring next to her.

"It's Willie!" she sighed.

Willie nudged Sofia's head.

"But both of you passed away. You can't be here, unless . . . unless I am in Cat Heaven."

"No such luck," I meowed. "You're still on Earth. You're in the hospital, Sofia."

"Then are you angels?" she asked as she gazed at our majestic wings.

"Yes, we are," Willie said proudly.

"I thought I felt you beside me when I was sick at home," she softly meowed. "I was dreaming and I couldn't move, but I knew two cat angels were helping me and were giving me my medicine. I woke up at the hospital."

"It was us, Sofia," Willie said.

"But what are you doing here?"

"We were sent from Cat Heaven to help you get better, and stay better," I meowed back.

Before Sofia could respond, she was carefully moved from the stretcher into a small carrying case. Then Sofia was transferred out of the big room.

Willie and I twitched our ears to the left and followed closely behind.

"What's going on?" Willie hissed.

"I'm not sure," I responded. We watched as the carrier was placed in the backseat of Valerie's vehicle. I signaled Willie to follow Sofia into the vehicle. Then we positioned ourselves on either side of the carrying case.

When the vehicle started up, Sofia began to meow.

"Don't worry," whispered Willie. "We are right here and will keep you safe."

"I think maybe Valerie is bringing me home," responded Sofia. "I recognize this vehicle. This may be a good sign."

"You must be on the road to recovery," I told her.

Soon Sofia fell asleep. Willie and I remained at her side.

I looked outside at the scenery. It was raining. I could see a lot of evergreen trees and houses. I thought about the cats living in those homes and what they might be doing, and whether they needed our help. But our mission was to help four cats, and Sofia was one of them. I looked back at the carrying case, where she was resting peacefully and sighing contently.

Valerie made a left turn, then a right, and finally I spotted my Earthly home. Valerie stopped the car and carried the case into the house. Willie and I flew directly behind.

Valerie opened the case and carefully lifted Sofia out. She hugged and soothed her. Valerie then put Sofia down gently. Sofia saw Muris and Lana lounging in the living room. Rather than approach them, she hurried into the bedroom, where she found her food dish. We watched Sofia gobble up the food and then slowly pace around the bedroom.

"Sofia," I meowed, "you must not gobble your food, especially after just being in the hospital."

Sofia didn't respond; she just kept pacing around in the room.

"She didn't hear you," Willie replied. "Sofia, are you feeling sick again?" he asked as he fluttered in front of her. Sofia sneezed and kept pacing around the room.

"Oh, dear," I meowed. "Sofia can't see or hear us now, and

we haven't had the chance to tell her about eating right and taking her medicine!"

"We'll have to use our golden dust so she can see us again," Willie said, pointing to my collar. Just then, loud cat meows sounded from my cat watch—fifteen minutes left.

"Hurry, Minka, we don't have very much time before we need to leave, and we still have some important things to explain to Sofia," Willie told me. He whooshed into the air, flicked his tail, made a few circles, pointed his paws down, and landed in front of Sofia.

Surprised by Willie's persistence, I reached for the golden dust around my collar. Tugging the sack open, I placed a small portion of golden dust on my right paw, made my wish, and sprinkled it over Sofia.

Immediately she stopped pacing and stared as a beautiful angelic glow filled the bedroom. As we fluttered our wings, the beautiful translucent mist flickered over Sofia.

Sofia turned to face us. "I knew you'd come back!"

"We don't have much time before we have to return to Cat Heaven," I meowed.

"You have to go back so soon?" Sofia looked anxious. "But I don't want you to leave! I'm scared I'll get sick again and you won't be here to help me."

"Sofia, listen to us," Willie interjected. "We've been sent from Cat Heaven to help you, and if you listen to what we say, you are sure to stay healthy."

Again, I was surprised by Willie's forthrightness. He was still rambunctious and excited about our adventures on Earth, but he had matured and become a very wise cat.

The loud cat meows sounded from my cat watch—ten minutes to go.

We spent our last few minutes with Sofia explaining what she could and couldn't eat, and how important it was to eat regularly and not hide under the bed when it was time for her insulin shots.

Sofia nodded. At my suggestion, she placed a few cat toys near her dish to remind herself to eat slowly. The toys would distract her from gobbling her food.

The loud cat meows sounded from my cat watch—five minutes left.

Sofia looked at the two of us, and at our wings. She seemed amazed at the way the feathers glowed to create a beautiful tapestry of colors—yellow as bright as the sun's rays, red as rich in color as roses, blue as serene and deep as the ocean, and gold shimmering magically.

"Thank you for saving my life," whispered Sofia. "I will miss your warmth and purrs. I wish we'd had more time together."

"We will someday," I told her softly.

"There will never be a day when I won't think of you both and what you have taught me. You are my angel heroes!" Sofia cried.

"We will live in your heart and always be beside you," Willie told her. "When you wake up in the morning and feel the warmth, it is our angel presence keeping you restful and safe."

"Sofia, stay healthy. I love you," I meowed as Willie and I positioned ourselves in front of Sofia. "Until we meet again," I whispered.

Sofia nodded. Then the two of us shouted, *"Brastic, astik!"* Off we flew through the fluffy gray clouds of the Earth's sky, into the fresh ozone layer of the Heavenly World, and safely back to our angel clouds.

We chanted our code in front of the guide helpers, and our wings disappeared from our backs. The guide helpers flew off into the distance, carrying our beautiful, glowing wings.

Willie and I looked at each other in pure contentment. Willie kneaded his angel cloud to find the perfect spot, yawned, and fell asleep. I lay down on my cloud, thinking about Sofia until my thoughts drifted into a deep sleep.

18. Zarah

I woke early the next morning and yawned, stretched, and kneaded my angel cloud. I peered down through my angel cloud and focused on finding my old home to see how Sofia was doing.

I saw that Sofia was at her food dish. Sofia seemed very engaged in her meal but was not gobbling her food. She would take a few bites and then look at her favorite toys, paw at them, and resume eating. To my delight, I saw she had gained back some weight. Sofia looked healthy and I felt very content.

Back on top of my angel cloud, I kneaded it until I found the perfect spot. I thought about the three cats Willie and I had visited. First, we taught Muris how to become friendlier with other cats and animals. Next, Willie and I helped Casper learn to stay at home and not wander around outside, where he could be in danger or get sick. Third, we helped Sofia learn to eat a better diet so that she wouldn't have too much sugar in her body. In the course of doing that, we saved her life. My Earthly wish was nearly complete.

The fourth cat we chose to visit was Zarah. If Zarah had been first on the list, I would have felt very anxious. I didn't know her well and was uncertain of what to do to help her, but at least now I had a sense of what might (or might not) happen during our trip to Earth.

I turned to face Willie's cloud. He was soundly sleeping. I sighed. We had become quite the team during our Earthly visits. Willie had matured, become a confident angel, and persevered in the face of danger. I, on the other hand, was still learning to let go of the need to be in control of every situation, and trying not to worry too much about the outcome. I had to trust my instinct and the angel force.

"Minka, did you sleep well?" asked Willie as he yawned and stretched.

"I did, Willie," I meowed.

"I'm hungry. I wonder if Sofia is hungry too," he remarked.

"She just ate," I reassured him.

"How do you know?" Willie asked as he sat upright.

"I watched from my angel cloud. There she was, right by her food dish," I remarked. "Sofia didn't gobble her food, but she enjoyed her meal as she played with her toys."

Willie smiled at me, did a somersault, and landed on the other end of his angel cloud.

"We have one more cat to visit," I reminded him.

"I know. We're going to visit Zarah, the beautiful young cat who moved into our neighborhood," he replied.

"What can we do to help her?" I asked Willie.

142

"Zarah is different, but in a good way. She is from a faraway place and meows differently than the rest of the cats in our neighborhood. The other cats tease and laugh at her," he explained. "We need to help them realize that she isn't any different than they are. In fact, Zarah probably has some great qualities she can teach the other cats."

I no longer felt amazed by Willie's self-assured poise. As I nodded in agreement, I saw Chloe and Oscar off in the distance flying toward us.

Oscar fluttered around Willie during his morning ritual: a lavish breakfast followed by a long bath. Willie jabbered away the entire time about flying to Earth, going to the animal hospital, hearing the beeping noises, and seeing the other sick animals. He told Oscar about finding Sofia on the stretcher, the car trip home, and how we taught Sofia about eating a good diet. Oscar would nod and ask Willie a question or two. After he brushed Willie's fur and cleaned behind his ears, he pampered Willie with a few catnip toys.

It was very different between Chloe and me. She provided me with a great breakfast followed by an oil-rich bath. But, in contrast to Oscar, she was very silent. I remained quiet as well. I could sense Chloe was in deep reflection. At first, I thought she might have been disappointed with our last trip to see Sofia.

Then it dawned on me that Chloe's silence was not about me, but about her. I had no idea what she had done for her Earthly wish or how she became an angel buddy. Still, I sensed that Chloe wished she could have done something similar to what Willie and I were doing: watching over our cat friends from Cat Heaven.

I looked at Chloe, who was clipping my nails. She paused a moment and then smiled at me.

"We will be back at midnight for your first trip to help Zarah," she stated as she gathered up the bathing supplies and nodded at Oscar to do the same. Before he left, Oscar nudged Willie on the forehead, and then he and Chloe flew off into the horizon.

As Willie and I watched our angel buddies fly away, we kneaded our angel clouds in preparation for a long catnap.

Willie and I slept the entire day. When midnight arrived, we both jumped up when we heard the loud *rat-ta-ta* flapping sound in the near distance. The glowing light from our beautiful wings brightened our angel clouds. First to land on our angel clouds were the guide helpers, followed by Chloe and Oscar.

"Are you two ready for your first trip to visit Zarah?" Oscar asked excitedly.

"Yep, ready to go!" meowed Willie.

"Good luck," nodded Chloe.

Willie and I positioned ourselves in our flight stance and shouted, *"Sastik, mastic, kulik, pelik, skeber, veber, milip, tips!"* Our heavenly wings appeared on our backs.

We both ran forward and shouted, *"Brastic, astik!"* and fluttered into the air.

Our angel wings quickly whooshed us to the left, and we descended through the fresh, clean ozone layer of the Heavenly World into the Earth's sphere. We traveled for miles until we reached the city of Seattle. Finally, we arrived at Zarah's house, which was a few doors down the street from my old Earth home.

Now Willie and I were in unknown territory. We had no idea about the layout of Zarah's home or how we were going to find her. We flew from room to room, not sure if we would encounter another cat, a dog, or an obstacle.

After not finding any creature in the house, Willie suggested we go outdoors.

We searched the backyard for Zarah, with no luck. I was getting anxious and knew our time was running out. I took a few deep breaths to calm myself and followed Willie over a fence into the front yard.

"There she is!" he shouted.

I looked where Willie was pointing. Zarah sat in the driveway looking in our direction. She was absolutely gorgeous.

Her coat was entirely gray except for a white marking on her chest. Zarah's fur was elegant and glimmered as though covered with angel dust. Her amber eyes were as opulent as amber stones from the Baltic Sea. I could tell Zarah was from a faraway place just by her lovely poise. She was worldly and full of grace, as though she was descended from royalty.

"So what do you want to do?" I asked Willie.

"Let's see how she interacts with the other cats in the neighborhood," Willie suggested.

Nodding, I fluttered over to where Zarah was sitting and positioned myself next to her.

Soon I noticed a neighborhood cat heading in Zarah's direction. Her gray tail twitched back and forth as she watched the cat approach.

As the cat came nearer, she let out a loud, low-voiced cry. I was a bit startled. Her voice was very unusual, as though she were singing. The neighborhood cat stopped in its tracks. Then he crouched low to the ground, hissed at Zarah, and ran in the other direction. Zarah stared after him, and then sadly twirled around in her spot.

"She does sound a bit strange," Willie admitted. "But it's kind of a pretty sound."

"As though she were singing," I agreed.

Zarah noticed two cats playing in the yard across the street from her house and quickly ran over to greet them. Again, she let out her loud, low-voiced meow to say 'hello' to them. The cats stopped what they were doing. Zarah twitched her tail back and forth, hoping the two cats would greet her as well. Instead, they closely surrounded her, trying to imitate her meow, and then hissed. One cat tried to scratch Zarah's head, but she darted the swat. The cats laughed and ran away.

Looking dejected, Zarah retreated down the driveway. She put her head down and slumped her shoulders.

The loud cat meows sounded from my cat watch—fifteen minutes to go.

"We don't have much time, Minka. I'm not sure we have accomplished very much during our first visit," Willie meowed, sounding disappointed.

"But we have, Willie. We observed what is upsetting Zarah," I reassured him. "That's a perfect start in figuring out how we may help her."

Willie looked puzzled.

"Do you have a plan?" he asked.

"I think so. I will explain when we get back to Cat Heaven," I replied. "But for now, let's sit close to Zarah. I have an instinctive feeling that the plan is about to unfold."

Willie and I spent our last few minutes beside Zarah. She sneezed at our presence but was no longer meowing. I could hear a beautiful song rising from her soul—a song that came from her

heart, one that would lead to fulfillment.

One thing was sure: I knew I wanted to be part of her song.

After we heard the last alarm from my cat watch, Willie and I positioned ourselves in our flight stance and shouted, *"Brastic, astik!"* Our angel wings spread open and off we flew through the city of Seattle, the fluffy white clouds of the Earth's sky, and the fresh ozone layer of the Heavenly World, back to Cat Heaven. The entire trip home I found myself floating and dancing, immersed in the song coming from my own soul.

When we arrived at our angel clouds, we chanted our code and our wings landed in front of the four guide helpers. They flew off into the distance, making their loud *rat-ta-ta* flapping sound and carrying our beautiful, glowing wings.

Willie and I fell asleep as soon as our heads hit our angel pillows.

19. Sing a Song

The next day was spent in our morning breakfast ritual followed by a long, lazy afternoon. Willie jumped over to my angel cloud, fully rested but anxious to hear my plan to help Zarah.

When I explained it, Willie's eyes opened wide. "Awesome!" he shouted as he twirled in the air and did a few somersaults. "But do we have enough angel dust to sprinkle Zarah?"

"Yes, I think so." I tugged at the sack around my collar. "Look!" The sack was still filled a quarter of the way with golden dust. "We can split the dust into a couple portions. We'll have enough for our second trip to help Zarah, and after that we can decide how to use the rest."

Willie nodded his agreement. I nudged his forehead. The two of us sat and waited on my angel cloud for midnight to arrive. We were a team, and we were determined to stick together.

When Chloe saw us, I knew she was about to say something.

Then Oscar nudged her. "Forget about the rules—let them be."

Chloe looked in the direction of the guide helpers, who were making their way toward our angel clouds. Their loud *rat-ta-ta* flapping sound echoed through the air.

"Are you ready?" asked Oscar.

"We are," I meowed back.

"Have a safe trip and call if you need my help," Chloe reminded me. She came over and whispered in my ear, "I am proud of both of you."

Willie and I positioned ourselves in our flight stance and shouted, *"Sastik, mastic, kulik, pelik, skeber, veber, milip, tips!"* Our heavenly wings appeared on our backs.

We both ran forward and shouted, *"Brastic, astik!"* and fluttered into the air.

Our angel wings quickly whooshed us to the left and we descended through the fresh, clean ozone layer of the Heavenly World. We traveled for miles in the Earth's atmosphere until we descended into the city of Seattle. We soon arrived at Zarah's home.

We found Zarah in the backyard, sitting near the swing set. She looked lonely. When we moved closer to her, she sneezed, but glanced around as though somehow she sensed our presence.

"I knew she was different," meowed Willie.

"Yes, she knows some magical force is nearby," I answered. "Zarah is in tune with outside forces. If you listen very carefully, you can hear the song that is coming from her soul."

Willie smiled. "It's a lullaby, coming from her heart!"

"That is the song that we want the other cats to hear," I replied.

Suddenly Zarah jumped onto one of the swings. She sat there, swaying, until the swing began to move. I reached for the golden dust around my collar. I tugged the sack open and placed a scant portion of the golden dust in my right paw. Then I sprinkled Zarah with the golden dust and made my wish.

Immediately, Zarah meowed. As Willie and I watched, she swayed back and forth to get the swing to move a bit more, grunted to clear her throat, and then began to meow her lullaby.

Willie and I swayed back and forth to the rhythm of her lullaby. Our wings spread wide and softly fluttered. The beautiful translucent mist flickered from our wings into the air.

Zarah's meowing became louder as she began singing from her heart. The song sounded like a mother cat singing to her newborn kittens. It wavered in the air, following the magical mist that flickered from our wings.

Willie seemed mesmerized. He kept staring at Zarah. I, too, was entranced, but I noticed a subtle change in the air. I felt the warmth that radiates from the Earth's atmosphere every so often. The air felt fresh and carried the scent of a summer day. From their nests in the trees, the birds started to chirp along with Zarah's melody. Even the trees swayed back and forth in tune. I felt as though Willie and I were back in Cat Heaven.

I saw two cats approaching the backyard. Moving cautiously, they stopped to listen to her song and then took a few more cat steps forward. They jumped over the fence and slowly approached the swing set. Then they sat directly in front of the swings, far enough away not to disturb Zarah's singing.

"They are coming," whispered Willie.

A third cat appeared in the backyard, followed by three more. They surrounded the swing set. Zarah continued to sway and sing

from her heart. She didn't seem to notice the cats who had encircled her. She was in her own trance. She was doing what she was meant to do, sharing her beautiful gift with the world.

Before long, a large group of cats had clustered around the swing set. The cats seemed entranced by Zarah's song.

"I have never seen such cat togetherness," I whispered to Willie. "It's as though they are one force, united to make the world a better place for cats."

"It's so cool. I wish I could have been part of something like this when I was on Earth," Willie said.

When Zarah finished her song, she gazed up at the sky. Some of the cats watching her began to whisper to each other. Zarah heard the whispering and looked over to see that her backyard was filled with cats.

She seemed startled by the sight. At first she didn't move, but then she quickly jumped down and sprinted over to hide behind a lounge chair.

"Why did she run and hide?" asked Willie. "Can't she see they want to know her?"

"That's just it, Willie. When she longed to find a friend, the cats in the neighborhood teased and laughed at her. Now she's unsure what they will do," I explained. "Zarah sang from her heart, and she doesn't want them to make fun of her singing."

The loud cat meows sounded from my cat watch—fifteen minutes left.

Just then, one of the cats headed toward Zarah. He was a calico and very sure of himself. He was probably the leader of the pack. Zarah moved back slightly and positioned herself farther under the chair.

"Hello, Zarah. My name is Felix," he stated loudly. "You have a lovely singing voice."

Slowly Zarah moved out from under the chair and began to purr quietly.

"We haven't been very nice to you, and I want to apologize for all of us. You are different from us, and perhaps we judged you too harshly," Felix went on.

Zarah's tailed swished back and forth, as though she were listening.

"Most of us have lived here all our lives. You came from someplace exotic and we didn't know how to respond to you," Felix explained. "We might have been jealous of your lovely presence in the neighborhood. It was easier to tease you than to get to know you."

"I'm not really that different," Zarah said. "I lived in Latvia. The cats in Latvia do the same kind of cat stuff that you all do. I just meow with an accent!"

"Yes, a strong, low accent!" Felix laughed.

Loud cat meows sounded from my cat watch—ten minutes to go.

"If you can find it in your heart, we would like to be your friends," Felix said.

"I would like that," Zarah responded.

I sighed and fluttered over to a rosebush to smell the fragrance from the flowers. I was feeling a bit of romance in the air. I twirled and danced around the rosebush. Willie was totally excited. He lifted his head, curled up his body, and did a few somersaults in the air. Then Willie pointed his paws and made a perfect landing next to Zarah.

"We would like to invite you to join our Secret Cat Clubhouse," Felix said proudly. "And to sing some more!"

"Well . . . okay," Zarah said shyly.

"Oh, this is so cool—a concert by Zarah!" Willie sounded excited. "I've always wanted to hear a concert! And play bass guitar in a rock band! This is awesome!"

The loud cat meows sounded from my cat watch—five minutes left.

"Yes, Willie, we have made a lot of headway, but there is some work left to be done," I replied.

"Like what?"

"There's the matter of Zarah's confidence, and whether she really wants to sing to all the other cats," I replied.

Willie looked confused.

"And what's all this about a rock group?" I said sternly. "I think we need to talk when we get back to Cat Heaven," I meowed. "It's time to go."

The two of us shouted, *"Brastic, astik!"* Off we flew through the city of Seattle, the fluffy white clouds, and the Earth's sky. I was still twirling and feeling a lot of love in the air. We entered the fresh ozone layer of the Heavenly World, and flew safely back to our angel clouds.

When we arrived at our angel clouds, the guide helpers were waiting for us. We chanted our code and our wings disappeared from our backs. The guide helpers flew off into the distance carrying our beautiful, glowing wings.

I instantly lay down on my angel cloud. But Willie kept fluttering all over his cloud, asking what I meant about Zarah's confidence.

"Let's rest tonight and talk tomorrow," I meowed sternly.

"But I want to be part of a rock band, and play bass guitar," Willie murmured until he, too, fell asleep.

20. Building Confidence

ate the next morning I woke to a loud strumming noise coming from Willie's angel cloud. I sat straight up with my tail twitching back and forth. Willie was sitting on his angel cloud playing a bass guitar! At first, I found the noise quite irritating, but after a while, I found the deep, low rhythm quite relaxing. Willie was playing his own tune, a reflection of newfound strength and character.

"Willie, where did you get the bass guitar?" I asked.

"Oscar brought it over early this morning," Willie called back. "You were sound asleep. I was wide awake and ready to start the day, but Chloe didn't want to disturb your sleep. I told them all about our trip, and they were entranced with my story. Before Oscar left, he asked if I needed anything, and I told him to get me a bass guitar."

"And what are you planning to do with it?" I asked as my tail started to twitch back and forth again.

"Play backup at Zarah's concert!" Willie shouted excitedly. "Look down—Zarah is trying to sing!"

I peered far down through my angel cloud to see Earth. I focused on finding Zarah and spotted her in the yard on one of the swings. She was slowly moving the swing back and forth. Instead of singing beautifully, she kept clearing her throat and then pitching a note and coughing. Just as I feared, Zarah was losing her nerve.

"Minka? Who are you staring at?"

It was Chloe. Startled, I popped my head back through my angel cloud. I hadn't noticed that Oscar and Chloe had arrived. Over on Willie's cloud, Oscar and Willie were jamming on bass guitars.

"I'm watching Zarah," I responded as my tail twitched back and forth.

"Willie told us about your trip to Earth. He said you were worried about Zarah and her upcoming concert," Chloe said. "Maybe I can help."

I kneaded my angel cloud and began telling Chloe that Zarah had sung beautifully but I was concerned she would lose her confidence and not want to perform.

"Zarah is a strong and spiritual cat, but at the same time she seems very fragile. She wants to be accepted by the cats in the neighborhood and fears they may not like her, even if she sings for them," I remarked. "Just now, she wasn't singing, only clearing her throat. I am not sure how we can help Zarah perform a concert if she hasn't practiced any songs. We don't have enough golden dust to create an entire concert!"

"You are very observant to notice Zarah's fears. Yes, she does seem hesitant to perform," remarked Chloe. "Zarah does not realize she has already gained the acceptance of the neighborhood cats,

and that they are simply looking forward to hearing her beautiful meowing again. Maybe she needs some encouragement from Felix!"

"Felix?"

"Yes—he likes her a lot, and she likes him, too!" Chloe smiled.

"Well, what can I do about that?" I meowed. "How can I help Zarah from my angel cloud?"

"You have angel powers you have not yet fully tapped. You and Willie helped Sofia without relying on the golden dust," Chloe informed me. "Simply do what you were doing before I interrupted you, and concentrate some more. Remember, your next trip is scheduled for midnight."

I wasn't quite sure what Chloe meant, but I knew that Chloe had the answer and was true in heart in supporting me. She turned to Willie's cloud.

"Oscar, the jam session is over—we need to go," she remarked sternly.

Oscar strummed a few more chords and then nodded at Willie. "Let's think about giving a concert at the Cat Heaven Auditorium," he meowed.

Chloe looked impatient. "Later, Oscar."

Oscar draped his bass guitar over his shoulder, and the two of them fluttered off toward the horizon.

Willie turned his concentration to writing another tune. While he was doing that, I needed to figure out what to do about Zarah and Felix.

I peered down through my angel cloud. Zarah was still sitting on the swing. She was looking at the ground, not even trying to sing. Next, I focused on finding Felix. I finally found him sitting in the driveway in front of Zarah's house.

Chloe was right—Felix liked Zarah. He was trying to find a way to get close to her. My tail twitched back and forth.

Chloe had told me to concentrate. I kept peering down at Zarah, and then at Felix. I kept my thoughts on the two of them. Felix could help Zarah's confidence by showing her that he accepted her and, even more than that, liked her. My thoughts fluttered about a romance between them. Maybe love did conquer all!

Suddenly, my tail started to twitch faster than it ever had before! The beautiful translucent mist flickered from my tail to circle around my cloud. The mist quickly swerved and whooshed down through the fresh, clean ozone layer of the Heavenly World, into the Earth's sphere, and through the city of Seattle to Zarah's home, where it grazed Felix ever so slightly.

Immediately he moved from the driveway and ran into the backyard. Zarah was still looking at the ground and didn't notice his presence.

"Hi, Zarah," Felix said softly. "I was wondering if you would like some company. Maybe I can help you figure out which songs to sing at the Secret Cat Clubhouse."

My tail swirled in circles. The translucent mist whooshed down through the Heavenly World and into the Earth's atmosphere, and then it touched Zarah ever so lightly.

Zarah smiled at Felix. "You can try," she said, "but I am not sure that I can even sing anymore."

"That's ridiculous!" exclaimed Felix. "Sure you can! Let me hear what you have been practicing."

My tail swirled in circles, and the beautiful translucent mist traveled the far distance from our world to theirs and touched Zarah again.

"I have to tell you the truth," Zarah said in a low voice. "I'm afraid the cats won't like me. It's made me lose my song."

"But I like you," Felix said. "And if I like you, the other cats will too! Start with the do-re-me stuff! In the Secret Cat Clubhouse, we saw a movie where seven kittens learned how to sing with their nanny. Before long, they were able to sing beautiful cat songs."

"Do-re-me . . ." sang Zarah.

"Excellent! Now try fa-so-la," Felix ordered.

"Fa-so-la," sang Zarah.

"Good, now you have some notes to sing. I bet you know the rest and can sing anything!" In answer, Zarah cleared her throat. She started to meow a tune softly. Her voice became louder as she meowed. Felix swayed to the rhythm of her song. Zarah ran to one side of the yard, stopped, and sang some more. Felix joined her and swayed some more. Zarah ran to the other side of the yard, stopped, and meowed even louder. Felix followed. For the rest of the day, the two played together as Zarah meowed various tunes.

Finally, they settled near the swing set. Felix licked Zarah's ears. She nudged his face and curled up next to him. Zarah softly meowed a lullaby, which eventually lulled them to sleep.

I smiled and popped my head back up through my angel cloud. I was exhausted but content. Now I knew that Willie and I were ready for our final trip to Earth.

I looked over at Willie, who was still jamming on his bass guitar. I had no idea how long I had been entranced by the sight of Zarah and Felix, but during that time Willie had composed another tune!

I kneaded my cloud and lay down for a long catnap. I fell asleep to the sound of Willie's strumming.

When I awoke, Chloe and Oscar were fluttering over our angel clouds. I could hear the loud *rat-ta-ta* flapping sound echoing through the air. The guide helpers were making their way toward our angel clouds. I quickly got up.

"Are you ready?" asked Oscar.

"I am," Willie meowed as he draped his bass guitar over his shoulder. "Minka still seems a bit groggy from her long catnap!"

"She's ready," remarked Chloe.

"Are you planning on flying with your bass guitar?" I asked Willie.

"We'll make an exception for your final trip," Chloe said as she came over to me and brushed my fur, making me presentable after my long nap.

Then she whispered in my ear, "You did a great job with Zarah and Felix. We have decided to let it all happen during your last trip to Earth! Be safe and have fun."

Willie and I positioned ourselves in our flight stance and shouted, *"Sastik, mastic, kulik, pelik, skeber, veber, milip, tips!"* Our heavenly wings appeared on our backs.

We both shouted, *"Brastic, astik!"* and fluttered up into the air. We were flying back to Earth on our final trip.

21. The Concert

We arrived at Zarah's home. The two of us quickly fluttered through the house. I had no thought of finding Zarah inside the house, but Willie and I made a quick scout just in case my hunch was wrong. "She's over here!" Willie shouted, pointing at the bedroom.

My heart sank, thinking that Zarah was hiding and had lost her confidence again. If that was the case, I had no idea what to do, since this was our last trip to Earth!

I found Zarah sitting in front of the mirror. She was licking her fur. Then she posed this way and that, meowing softly, pouncing to the rhythm of her song, and watching herself in the mirror.

"Look, she's practicing her moves," meowed Willie.

"She sure is, and she looks beautiful!" I exclaimed.

Zarah practiced a bit longer and then decided it was time to head outdoors. Willie and I followed. Zarah ran to the backyard and jumped on one of the swings. She kept staring at the backyard fence. Her tail began to twitch back and forth.

I looked at the fence in time to see Felix jump over it. He quickly ran over to her. Zarah jumped from the swing and the two of them nudged each other's heads. "Are you ready for your concert?" Felix asked affectionately.

Zarah purred and nudged Felix's head. "I think so."

They crossed the lawn, jumped over the fence, and headed in the direction of the Secret Cat Clubhouse.

Willie positioned his bass guitar across his shoulder and nodded for me to follow them. Lifting our heads up, we flew over the rooftops and then pointed our paws down to land outside the Secret Cat Clubhouse.

No other cats had arrived yet. Zarah had an hour to warm up her voice onstage. As soon as Willie and I entered the party room, we stopped in awe. The large room had been decorated with colored balloons, all in the shape of cats. Yellow, pink, blue, and green streamers hung from the shaded windows. Twenty round tables were arranged symmetrically around the room. A few tables were close to the stage. At the center of each table was a small, carved cat post, and on top of each post was a softly glowing light.

Two long tables had been set up on the left side of the room. One had an assortment of cat food, and the other held small water dishes. In the center of the ceiling a crystal disco ball revolved, capturing the rays from the glowing table lights. Rays of color shimmered onto the walls and ceiling of the party room.

Willie nudged me. "This is truly amazing!"

"It looks like they're expecting at least two hundred cats!" I meowed. I, too, was amazed at the effort that had gone into preparing for Zarah's concert.

I saw Zarah follow Felix onto the stage. With his

encouragement, she started to practice a few of her songs. Her meows were in perfect pitch and mesmerizing. Still, something was missing.

Before I could say a word, Willie pulled his bass guitar from his shoulder and began strumming along to Zarah's song. It was the perfect addition. I thought about what Chloe had said before we left: "We have decided to let it all happen during your last trip to Earth."

I watched Zarah sing and move about the stage and then glanced at Willie, who was accompanying her on his guitar. I pawed at the sack around my collar, tugged it open, and checked to see how much golden dust was left inside.

As cats began to arrive, Felix whooshed Zarah below the stage to the celebrity dressing room. I signaled Willie to stop playing, and we followed the two downstairs.

The dressing room was lined with mirrors. A large makeup table and chair were placed in the center of the room. There were grooming combs, collars, and cat-safe makeup. Zarah went to sit in the chair. She licked and brushed her fur.

"I'll stay here until the organizers announce that it's time to go onstage," meowed Felix.

Willie and I heard a lot of hubbub upstairs. Cats were arriving and socializing before the concert. I was getting quite excited, as was Willie, who was fluttering around the dressing room.

Zarah was looking at herself in the mirror. She accented her eyes with cat eyeliner and dabbed some cat gloss on her whiskers. Felix kept close guard at the door.

There was a knock on the door. Two cat organizers stood there. "It's time," one said.

Felix nudged Zarah's forehead and licked her ears. The two of them left the dressing room and dashed up the stairs. Willie and I followed.

Behind the drawn curtains, Zarah positioned herself in the center of the stage. Felix stood in the wings next to where the curtains would be opened. Willie and I stood behind Felix.

One of the organizers trotted across the stage, hushed the crowd, and announced Zarah's performance. As the curtains began to rise, I looked at Willie. "Go on—take your place behind Zarah."

Willie looked excited. "Really?" he asked. I nodded, and Willie quickly fluttered over behind Zarah. Then I reached for my collar. I tugged the sack open and placed the remaining portion of the golden dust in my right paw. I sprinkled Zarah with the golden dust and made my wish.

Suddenly an entire cat rock band appeared behind Zarah, with Willie in front.

The audience applauded wildly as the rock band began to play. Zarah slowly looked around. She let out a soft meow and then turned to face the cat audience.

Finally, Zarah began to sing. The cat rock band accompanied her in perfect harmony. Willie led the band with the rhythm of his bass guitar, even though none of the band members or the audience could see him. They could only hear the beat vibrate throughout the room.

Zarah's voice was mesmerizing. The cat audience grew silent, listening to her beautiful song. I stood behind Felix, who was enthralled with the music and swayed back and forth to the beat. I, too, swayed as my wings quietly fluttered.

At the end of her song, Zarah turned and bowed to her band as the audience clapped their paws.

The concert lasted over an hour. Zarah's song selection was

ideal for the occasion—gentle, pure, and heartfelt. The message she conveyed was about cat unity and togetherness, loving one another despite differences, and finding love. There were many tears shed in the audience. Felix seemed very touched by her songs. I sensed he was falling deeply in love with Zarah.

Zarah also sang a few songs that had a samba beat. During these songs, she moved her hips and danced across the stage in a rhythmic beat. I, too, danced to the music and even did a few salsa moves. Willie went wild during the samba songs and did a few long solos. He leaped across the stage, pointing his guitar at the audience. He jammed chords and did some advanced picking techniques with smooth scale progressions. The beat from his guitar penetrated the party room. Willie was in ecstasy—totally in awe of his own musical abilities!

Zarah dedicated her last song to her newfound friends. She told the audience that she wrote this song when she first arrived in the Pacific Northwest, entering a new home with a fresh start in life. The lyrics were all about finding comfort in this new land and feeling accepted. The cat audience listened in silence, and then meowed wildly when Zarah finished singing. Zarah bowed and blew kisses to the audience. The cat audience demanded two encores.

Finally, the curtains closed. Zarah nudged each of the cat rock band members and then looked around for the bass guitarist and asked for his whereabouts. None of them played the bass or knew whom she was talking about.

When Felix nudged Zarah to return to the dressing room, she trotted down the stairs. Willie stood in the middle of the stage while the band members packed up their instruments. I fluttered over to him. "I was impressed with how well you played."

Willie looked around the stage tearfully. "The concert is over," he said sadly. "I never had the chance to play bass guitar when I was living on Earth."

"I know. We don't always have the chance to do everything we want to during our lifetime on Earth—but we can have that chance in Cat Heaven," I responded softly as my tail swished back and forth. "If I remember correctly, Oscar mentioned something about you two giving a performance at the Cat Heaven Auditorium."

Willie immediately perked up. "That's right, he did! Boy, oh, boy, I can't wait to tell him about my jam session during Zarah's concert. I bet he'll be impressed and will want to practice for our concert in Cat Heaven!"

"I'm sure he will!" I exclaimed. "Now let's go enjoy the party before we have to leave." I nudged Willie to follow me to where all the cats were socializing.

Several tables had been moved to make room for a dance floor. Cat tunes were playing from speakers installed next to the stage. Willie immediately trotted over to a group of cats who were engrossed in conversation. He tried to add his own thoughts, even though none of the other cats could hear them. That didn't seem to bother Willie.

I fluttered over to the far corner of the party room and stood on top of one of the round tables, from where I could watch all the action. My angel wings were fluttering softly.

When Zarah and Felix arrived, all the cats began to applaud. When they reached the center of the room, Felix stated that he had an important announcement to make. "Zarah and I are engaged," he exclaimed.

There were wild cheers. The cats surrounded the new couple to congratulate them.

After all the cats had given them their best wishes, Willie fluttered over to Zarah and softly nudged her. She shook her head, sneezed, and then saw Willie.

"It was you! You were my bass guitarist," she whispered. "Thank you for being there for me." Willie fluttered into the air, curled his body tight, and did a few somersaults.

From the table I watched all the cats mingling, feeling very sentimental. It was our last time on Earth. I gazed at all the vibrant decorations and the cats chattering. A few were dancing in the center of the party room. I pawed at the table, peered at the softly glowing lights, and sniffed the wonderful scents. I definitely would miss Earth.

The loud cat meows sounded from my cat watch and pulled me out of my trance—fifteen minutes to go. I looked over at Willie. He was in the middle of the dance floor, dancing to a top-hit Latino cat song. Watching him, I thought back over our long journey. I remembered our visits to help Muris, my partner during my life on Earth. I recalled how Willie became determined to save Casper from roaming the streets, and how much the two of them missed each other. Then there was Sofia. I remembered how Willie and I worked as a team to save her life. We were both very scared, yet our angel powers pulled us through.

All these trips were more than I could have ever imagined. I had tapped into my angel powers, even as Willie had a chance to tap into his talents.

Loud cat meows sounded from my cat watch and startled me—ten minutes left on Earth.

Willie was dancing in the center of a group of cats. I quickly fluttered over to him. I tried to get his attention and pointed at my watch. He ignored me and kept dancing. I grabbed Willie by the neck and yanked him over to the side of the party room.

"Willie, we're leaving. Get yourself together for our flight back to Cat Heaven," I meowed sternly.

"It's time to go already?" asked Willie.

"Yes, home to Cat Heaven."

Willie suddenly realized he was leaving and that his place was no longer on Earth. He pawed at the ground, did a few quick circles, looked around the party room, took a deep breath, and then looked at me. "You're right," he said quietly. "It's time to go home."

The two of us took our flight stance and shouted, *"Brastic, astik!"*

We fluttered into the air. Our angel wings quickly whooshed us to the left, and then, as fast as the speed of light, we departed from our old neighborhood. Willie kept looking back until he could no longer see it. Tears fell from his eyes.

We traveled south along the interstate and kept ascending high above the city of Seattle, where the two of us had lived our cat lives on Earth. I could see the Space Needle, the busy waterfront with ferries traveling to and from the San Juan Islands, and even the floating bridges. Willie kept gazing back at the city. He pawed at the sky, trying to slow our travel speed, but our angel wings kept carrying us farther upward until, with a quick left turn, we reached the fluffy white clouds.

I looked down at Earth for any landmarks, but we were traveling too fast to make sense of the land below us. I blew a kiss as I watched Earth become smaller and smaller and finally disappear from sight. We left the atmosphere and traveled a long distance into the fresh, clean ozone layer of the Heavenly World. Willie peered ahead, no longer trying to paw at the air. He knew we had left Earth forever.

We began to descend as we reached the gates of Cat Heaven.

We made a perfect landing on our angel clouds. Our angel wings vanished. Willie pawed at his angel cloud and circled until he found a resting spot. He instantly fell asleep.

I looked at him sleeping soundly, nudged at my angel cloud, and found my resting spot. Tears filled my eyes. Our Earthly wish had been completed. I wanted to return to Earth again, but our time on Earth had ended. Cat Heaven was our home.

Part Three—Cat Angels

22. Angel Castle

The next morning Chloe and Oscar appeared at our angel clouds while Willie and I were still asleep. They decided to return later. A busy afternoon was in store for us.

I kept dreaming about Earth. *I was playing with Muris on his deck. We nudged each other, and then jumped up on the railing of the deck. We leaped over the flowerpot and looked in the oak tree for a bird's nest. There we found Casper making his way down one of the branches. Casper jumped down from the deck railing, leaped on top of one of the lounge chairs, and positioned himself for a catnap. Sofia appeared at the dining room sliding door. It was closed. She pawed and pawed until she was able to slide the door open. Sofia ran over to where Casper was lounging. She jumped onto the lounge chair next to Casper. After Sofia took her medicine, she stretched and settled down for her catnap. Muris and I ran across the deck railing and looked out into the backyard. Zarah was in the middle of the yard, singing her lullaby. I swayed back and forth to her rhythm*—until I found myself nearly rolling off my angel cloud.

Quickly I leaped into the air and landed in the middle of my cloud. I looked over at Willie and saw him rolling around in his angel cloud. More than likely he was dreaming about dancing the rumba or playing his bass guitar.

"Willie," I whispered, "are you dreaming about being back on Earth?"

Willie yawned and stretched. "Yeah, I was having a great dream about being the leader of a famous cat rock band! We were playing at the Secret Cat Clubhouse. There was a huge turnout of cats. They were meowing wildly during my solo on the bass guitar. I looked really cool in my cat sunglasses!"

"We had some awesome experiences during our time on Earth," I exclaimed.

"I wish we could go back," sighed Willie, "but I know that our time spent on Earth helping our friends has come to an end. Cat Heaven is our home now. They need us here."

Just then Chloe and Oscar appeared at our angel clouds with an assortment of food.

"I see that you are awake," Chloe said. "We don't have much time before we have to fly you over to the Angel Castle. Be sure to eat plenty, because I don't know when we will return."

Willie and I immediately devoured the food. We were very hungry after spending so much energy during our last visit on Earth.

"Why do we have to go to the Angel Castle?" Willie asked while Oscar brushed his fur.

"The Angel Leaders are going to give a final evaluation of your Earthly wish and the time you spent on Earth as angel cats," Chloe told him as her tail swished back and forth.

"Don't worry. Everything went really well," Oscar added quickly.

Willie did a few somersaults in the air and landed next to Oscar.

"Don't get too excited until you meet with the Angel Leaders," Chloe meowed. "They will be reviewing all your Earth trips. Each visit will be scrutinized. The Leaders are going to be strict in their evaluation."

As Chloe began to groom me for our visit with the Angel Leaders, I turned to face her. "Will we meet the Leaders today?"

"I don't honestly know," she answered. "This is all new territory for me."

While Chloe was grooming me, I thought back to when I first arrived in Cat Heaven. Chloe had greeted me at the Doors of Cat Heaven and guided me to my angel cloud. Her voice was warm and purring. I remembered that she remarked how beautiful I was, with my soft white and black fur and hazel eyes. In the beginning I wasn't sure what to make of Chloe. As time passed, I realized I was really a lot like her—strong and strict, yet gentle and pure. It was Chloe who supported this wild dream I had about traveling to Earth. She had made it all happen with the Angel Leaders. If my journey in Cat Heaven had been remarkable, it was because of Chloe—she was now one of my dearest friends.

In the distance I could hear the *rat-ta-ta* wings of the guide helpers traveling toward our angel clouds. Chloe and Oscar left immediately and flew north. As soon as the guide helpers appeared, one clutched Willie by the neck and started to fly in the direction of the Angel Castle. The other guide helper lifted me up by the neck and quickly followed.

I peered at the angel clouds glowing magically below. They

went on for miles and miles. As we left the part of Cat Heaven that housed all cats, we traveled through large patterns of mystical clouds. The sky was filled with a shimmering light. I sensed a peacefulness and magic in the air, and a force resembling the power of Cat Heaven.

Off in the distance, the large and shimmering Angel Castle appeared, sitting on top of a huge, radiant, magical cloud. As we drew closer, I could see each of the cat scratching posts that were attached to the main castle. There were purple and violet cat posts, blue and turquoise posts, teal and green posts, red and orange posts, and finally pink and fuchsia posts. Shimmering stars circled around each post. Golden sparkles flickered from the large yellow cat post in the center, as well as from the golden fence that encircled the Angel Castle.

Our guide helpers flew Willie and me to the golden gates of the Angel Castle. Chloe and Oscar were there to greet us. "You had a safe flight," stated Chloe. "The two of you will be entering the Angel Castle with Oscar and me. This has never been allowed before. Do not say a word—rather, follow closely behind." Chloe nodded to the guide helpers, who departed quickly.

Chloe pressed the intercom at the entrance, and the large golden gate slowly opened. A large translucent cloud covered the red-brick pathway and filled the air around us. Willie and I trotted closely behind Chloe and Oscar.

The brick path led us to the main entrance of the Angel Castle. The sights, sounds, and smells were breathtaking. Vibrant tropical flowers, lush bushes, and trees lined the path. The fragrance radiating from the flowers was fresh and soothing. Palm, oak, maple, and cherry trees swayed in the soft wind. Bluebirds, yellow jacks, and red robins were chirping beautiful melodies from the trees. Waterfalls trickled into a translucent blue pond that was decorated

with shiny rocks and had colorful fish swimming all around in it.

I paused to sniff one of the flowers. Chloe's tail swished back and forth gently to remind me to stay close behind her. Willie was making a funny clicking noise with his mouth as he stared at the birds up in the trees and the fish swimming in the pond. He was about to leap into the pond when Oscar clutched his neck and turned him back to the red-brick path.

Finally we reached the entrance to the Angel Castle. The main door was pure gold, and in its center, a white-marble cat sat atop a cat post. It was looking in the direction of the sky and had angel wings and a halo.

When Chloe rang the bell, Willie and I were startled to hear loud cat meows. An angel cat servant opened the large golden door. He was pure black with a white goatee. He had a white bow tie around his neck and white gloves on his front paws.

The cat servant nodded and stated, "Please follow me." He led the four of us through a foyer lavishly decorated with white-marble cat posts. Around each were statues of different-colored cats playing together with happy expressions on their faces. The statues portrayed a feeling of togetherness. The walls of the foyer were decorated with paintings of beautiful cat scenes. One showed several cats looking up at a bird's nest, while another showed cats playing with a ball of yarn and looking into a small fishbowl. There were paintings of mother cats tending their little ones. They reminded me of Earth.

The four of us were guided to a theater on the first floor of the Angel Castle. There were only two rows with four seats in each row, all of which faced a wide plasma screen.

"Please take your seats," the cat servant directed, showing us to the front row of seats.

Chloe took her place at the end of the row. I sat next to her.

Willie sat next to me, and Oscar took his place next to Willie.

The four of us waited silently for the next event to happen.

"Good afternoon, Chloe, Oscar, Minka, and Willie," a low meow echoed throughout the theater.

Willie and I were startled and clung to each other.

"We, the Angel Leaders, are here to review Minka and Willie's Earthly wish," the low cat voice continued. "This wish has been quite an ordeal for us, the Leaders. We have put an immense amount of time and effort into your wish, from building your wings to teaching you how to fly and testing your ability."

Willie and I were trembling in our seats.

"We, the Leaders, also provided you with a set of guidelines to complete your Earthly wish. Your first rule was selecting the four cats to protect on Earth. You accomplished this by identifying cats in need of help, the second rule. The third rule was met by visiting each cat three times, for only four hours at a time. Neither of you surpassed your time limit during any of the visits. Bravo! The fourth rule was that if the cat was truly helped during your visits, they would sense or see some Heavenly vision of you. The fourth rule was accomplished as well."

Willie and I held each other's paws tightly.

"The final rule is why we are here today," the low cat voice added. "We, the Leaders, will review each of your flights, and afterward we will ask you why you did what you have done for your friends."

Immediately, the room darkened. Cat commercials were projected onto the plasma screen. Willie liked them, especially the one showing two cats chasing each other around a flowerbed. Both cats came to a screeching halt when they sniffed the organic cat food served in their cat dishes. The commercial reminded the cats to eat healthy so they would have enough energy to play.

There was a brief pause, and then our first visit to Earth was exhibited on the movie screen. Willie's eyes widened as he saw himself flying through the clouds while descending through the fresh, clean ozone layer of the Heavenly World and into the Earth's atmosphere, through the city of Seattle, over our Earth homes, and into my old bedroom. He chuckled when he saw the two of us tiptoe to the door leading to the hallway.

I buried my head in my paws. I couldn't watch the scene in which Willie and I peered around the door and saw Muris lounging in the middle of the hallway. I knew what happened during the remainder of that visit.

The review of our visits to Earth went on for a very long time. Every scene was carefully analyzed. If there was a question or concern by an Angel Leader about our actions, the scene was rewound and watched again.

I felt nervous watching our movies. Even though Willie and I had good intentions, we sometimes didn't make the best choices, particularly on the first visits with Muris and Casper. Instead of watching, I buried my head in my paws or clutched Willie's paw tightly. Yet, there were moments when I felt very proud, especially the scene in which we saved Sofia's life. I smiled and nudged Willie. The last few episodes of helping Zarah were awesome. It was amazing to see how Willie and I had tapped into our angel powers to help Zarah realize her gift. Willie was nearly in ecstasy as he watched himself perform onstage.

After the last visit to Earth finished, the lights in the theater came up. The four of us sat silently and waited nervously for the next announcement.

23. Synergy

Finally, a very old, distinguished-looking calico cat stepped out from behind the plasma screen. He was exquisitely handsome, like royalty. The calico cat had very large gold-feathered wings and a gold halo on top of his head. As he trotted across the stage, his golden wings released an abundance of golden sparkles that engulfed his entire body and then scattered through the air.

"Is he one of the Angel Leaders?" I whispered.

Chloe nodded.

When the calico reached the middle of the stage, he cleared his throat and said, "We have reviewed Minka and Willie's visits to Earth to help their cat friends. We have made our final report. Before we share the results with you, we need to ask Minka and Willie why their Earthly wish was important for them to complete."

I nervously looked at Willie and then at Chloe. Chloe nudged me. "Go to the stage and stand directly in front of the calico Angel Leader, and tell him why you did what you have done for your friends," Chloe whispered.

I slowly made my way past Willie and Oscar and walked up the side stairs to the stage. I trotted over to stand in front of the calico cat.

I paused for a few seconds, thinking of what I would say, yet my heart knew the truth. There was no hiding it, because I was in Cat Heaven and standing in front of an Angel Leader. I cleared my throat and spoke up shyly. "At first, when I had my idea of visiting Earth again, my intentions were selfish." I heard Chloe, Oscar, and Willie shuffle in their seats. "I wanted to see my steadfast partner during my life on Earth. I wanted to spend time with Muris again because I missed him so very much. I had a good, long life with Muris," I softly meowed.

The calico nodded. "Go on."

"During my time on Earth, I knew his temperament and that he wasn't very nice to the other animals who lived with us. I didn't pay much attention to his behavior because he was always very good to me," I explained. "Yet I knew that Muris was in need of my assistance to become a friendly cat and to purify the remainder of his existence on Earth. During our first visit, my worst fears were confirmed. As an angel, I was able to see how unkind he was to Lana and Sofia. It almost broke my heart."

I heard Chloe, Oscar, and Willie shuffle some more in their seats.

"I felt complete after Willie and I helped Muris. Maybe it was a way for me to say a last thank you to the partner who always kept me safe on Earth. Yet, even after our visits with Muris, I still didn't realize why it was important to help the other three cats. With Casper, I realized he was in danger of being hurt while roaming the streets, but the truth of the matter was, I was there for Willie. He needed to find closure with Casper." I turned to look at Willie, who was practically teary eyed.

"It wasn't until our visits to help Sofia that I felt a small, continuous calling in my heart. Somehow Willie and I saved Sofia's life. That was when I realized how much I wanted her to have the same long life I had. I wanted to give her that chance. At that moment, I knew it was my angel calling to serve other cats on Earth, giving my friends and other cats the protection and love they needed. I know I can't save every cat, and they can't all have a long life—that's not the way it works. But if there is even a chance to provide a cat with happiness or hope for even a day, that's what I am meant to do as an angel."

I turned to look at my friends. Oscar and Willie were sniffling; Chloe had tears in her eyes. "Zarah's visits proved the genuine purpose of my Earthly wish. I didn't know her well, yet Willie and I were able to help her find happiness," I meowed. "That is what I am meant to do from Cat Heaven. By helping cats on Earth, I felt an authentic happiness in my angel soul."

I stopped and looked into the eyes of the calico Angel Leader. They were very kind. An abundance of golden sparkles shot from his golden wings into the air.

"Thank you, Minka," he said. I turned around and went back to my seat.

"Willie, please approach the stage and let us hear your account of why your Earthly wish was important for you to complete," the calico requested.

Willie nervously nudged past Oscar and approached the stage.

"Ahem," Willie cleared his throat. "Well, my first reason for visiting Earth was because I thought it would be really cool to fly and also to see my best friend Casper again. I guess, like Minka's, my reasons were not very good at first. During our first visits, I had a blast doing somersaults in the air. It was a lot of fun jumping over Muris, making him sneeze, and him not seeing me. The mother bird thing was awesome."

Oscar chuckled. Chloe shushed him to be quiet.

"But when I saw Casper again, I got very sad. I thought about how I ended up in Cat Heaven, and I didn't want the same thing to happen to Casper before his time," Willie explained earnestly. "During our visits to Casper, there was danger looming in the streets. Minka and I had to help Casper stay safely indoors."

I looked over at Oscar. He looked very tearful listening to Willie's account. I wondered if he was thinking of his own friends back on Earth.

"It was during our last visit to help Casper that something came over me. I felt really connected to being an angel cat. I had a plan for Casper—I was determined and did everything in my angel powers to save him. I felt very proud that we gave my best friend the chance to live a longer life. It was really exciting when Casper saw me as an angel. He was in awe of my beautiful wings and promised me he would remain safe."

I looked over at Chloe. She was staring at Willie then Oscar, who was pawing the tears from his eyes.

"I grew stronger and more sure of my angel abilities during our trips to visit Sofia. Minka and I worked as a team to save Sofia's life. But the most fun was helping Zarah!"

The calico Angel Leader chuckled.

"I guess I grew up. I learned I had the dedication and perseverance to believe in and complete our Earthly wish. I learned that I was fully committed to helping our friends. For the first time

I was able to keep my attention focused on something other than me," Willie admitted.

"Thank you, Willie," the calico said. "Return to your seat. I will be back shortly with our final report."

As he trotted offstage, more golden sparkles released from his golden wings and shot into the air.

The four of us sat in our seats. None of us looked at each other or made a sound.

In a short time, the calico cat reappeared from behind the movie screen. "Minka and Willie, you two encountered many challenges during your trips to Earth. Yet you followed the four sacred rules. You also gave touching accounts about the final sacred rule—the most important rule of your Earthly wish. We, the Angel Leaders, feel your motives, though not entirely pure to begin with, were worthy of angel cats. Thus we, the Angel Leaders, have decided to give your Earthly wish a favorable report."

Willie leaped from his seat. Oscar grabbed him with his front paws and began licking his face. Chloe looked at me with a soft smile, meowed, and nudged my face.

I felt at peace.

"May I have your attention?" the calico said, interrupting the celebration. "We have some important announcements to make."

Willie and Oscar sat down, and we focused our attention on the calico Angel Leader.

"We, the Angel Leaders, have been inspired by Minka and Willie's Earthly wish and feel that there is room to formally expand your wish to other angel cats in Cat Heaven. We, the Leaders, have decided to create a new program called Friend Watch. It will be available to all angel cats in need of completing their Earthly wish before ascending to Higher Cat Heaven."

Willie and I nudged each other. Chloe and Oscar stared at each other in amazement.

"Angel cats interested in completing their wish by flying down to Earth to help other cats will inform their angel buddy. We, the Leaders, are aware that the list will be long. However, there will be strict standards regarding which angel cats may complete this wish. Once these standards are met, the angel cats will receive their wings and must pass a few tests before gaining approval to fly down to Earth."

Chloe raised her hand. "Will the angel buddies get training? Because, I have to say, Oscar and I went through quite a bit of stress—"

"Yes, all the angel buddies will receive training," replied the calico. "I am sure you have many questions, and we intend to address all of them. We, the Angel Leaders, will be arranging angel buddy meetings to explain the standards of this new program."

Chloe sat down, looking satisfied, though her tail swished back and forth.

"We, the Angel Leaders, believe this program will be an extension of the goodwill we teach our angel cats in Cat Heaven," stated the calico Angel Leader. "We hope that with the new program, all cats on Earth will benefit from having an angel watching over them—a synergy effect."

"What's synergy?" Oscar wanted to know.

The calico Angel Leader smiled. "It's something that's more than the power of one. Picture all the angel cats using their powers to help our cat friends on Earth."

Oscar looked at Chloe and the two of us, to see if we understood the Angel Leader's message.

"We, the Leaders, will hold a meeting next week at the

Cat Heaven Auditorium. We feel that Chloe and Oscar honor the program's intention by having been through this experience firsthand," the calico cat announced. "Minka and Willie's wings will be displayed at the meeting."

Oscar looked like he was about to faint. Willie licked Oscar's forehead and held his paw. I was so proud of Chloe and Oscar that I couldn't wait to leave so we could celebrate.

"Just one more announcement," the Angel Leader added. "We were very moved by Minka and Willie's efforts and the bravery they showed during their visits to Earth. That's why we have decided to grant Minka and Willie any position they desire in Cat Heaven. You will have a week to inform Chloe and Oscar of your choices."

Chloe looked at me, wide-eyed. When Willie turned to Oscar, he saw he had fainted.

The calico Angel Leader raised his paw and released an abundance of golden sparkles that swirled in the air and then around Willie and me. Before we could even blink, we were magically returned to our angel clouds, where we instantly fell asleep.

24. All Cats Go to Heaven

During the next week, the usual activities continued in Cat Heaven. As new angel cats would enter the Doors of Cat Heaven, their guide helpers would fly above them with a loud *rat-ta-ta* of flapping wings and point the cats out to their angel buddies. The angel buddies would take over and settle the new cats onto their assigned angel clouds.

Angel cats in Cat Heaven went on with their normal routines. Some munched on heavenly treats while others chased birds around their angel clouds. Angel cats pounced on mice, and cats learned the ropes from their angel buddies while others contemplated their Earthly wishes.

Willie and I kept to ourselves. We didn't talk much and didn't need to. Willie and I had been on a great journey together. We needed time to recuperate and recapture all the moments of our time on Earth, and—most of all—decide which positions we would choose in Cat Heaven.

Chloe and Oscar only visited during mealtimes. They, too, were very quiet. Once I heard Chloe ask Oscar if he was preparing a speech for the meeting. Oscar nodded and whispered in Chloe's ear.

I climbed a tree near my cloud to watch the birds chirping their angel melodies from their nests. I had a perfect view of the angel bees and butterflies flying around the flowerbeds. I thought about the birds, bees, and butterflies on Earth and how similar, yet different, they were to the ones here in Cat Heaven. They all got along in Cat Heaven, without territorial fighting or aggression toward one another.

I climbed higher, thinking about the different positions I'd like to have in Cat Heaven. I lifted my nose to the air and smelled the fresh scent of the Heavenly sky. I remembered the last time I'd sniffed all the scents of Earth, after Zarah's concert.

I definitely missed Earth.

Looking down, I peered as far as I could through the vast banks of angel clouds to see if I could visualize Earth from the tree. I gazed at the clouds for a long time, but all I could see was a fine trace of Earth.

That's when it hit me. I made my decision. I knew what I needed to do in Cat Heaven.

At last, the day arrived of the great meeting. Chloe and Oscar woke us early.

"I hope you slept well," stated Chloe. "We have time to give you a full breakfast followed by a lavish oil bath before we head over to the Heavenly Cat Auditorium. Have you decided yet on your position in Cat Heaven?"

Willie whispered in Oscar's ear. Oscar jumped for joy around Willie's angel cloud.

Then I turned to Chloe and whispered in her ear.

Chloe stopped still in amazement. Finally, she nudged my forehead and gave me an approving smile.

Oscar seemed very playful as he fed Willie breakfast and gave him his bath. The two laughed and nudged each other. On the other hand, Chloe was very quiet. She served me breakfast and made sure I had plenty to eat. She then prepared my bath and spent time lathering my fur and skin with oils and soap. After she had rinsed the oil and soap from my coat, she carefully brushed my fur to perfection.

"I am so proud of you, Minka," Chloe whispered. "I knew you were an extraordinary cat when I first greeted you at the Doors of Cat Heaven. I had a strong hunch I would experience something very profound, and my instincts were right. In fact," she said, "you are an ordinary cat who has extraordinary passion and kindness, and that's what makes you a hero."

I didn't know what to say. I looked at Willie.

"It's time," Chloe said.

Oscar clutched Willie by the neck and flew off in the direction of the Heavenly Cat Auditorium. Chloe and I followed closely behind.

As soon as we arrived at the Heavenly Cat Auditorium, we passed through the grand foyer and into the huge auditorium. Willie and I followed Chloe and Oscar as they trotted up to the stage and slipped behind the curtains.

In the middle of the stage was a wide plasma screen. To the right of the screen stood two red and gold chairs, and to the left, our wings. They were displayed in large glass cases, spread open to their fullest. Each feather glowed and created a beautiful tapestry of colors—yellow finch feathers, red robin feathers, and bluebird feathers. The golden seagull feathers sparkled brightly and gave our wings their magical and heavenly appearance.

Chloe pointed to the two royal chairs. "Take your seats. All the other cats, along with their angel buddies and guide helpers, will be arriving shortly."

Willie and I jumped onto the chairs and circled into our places. I felt nervous and excited at the same time. I saw Chloe and Oscar greet two pure-white angel buddies who had arrived on the stage. They didn't seem alarmed by our angel wings or the sight of us sitting in the royal chairs. They must have heard our story at one of the mandatory meetings for all angel buddies.

Chloe and Oscar pointed to the curtains, the lighting above the plasma screen, our wings, and finally at us. All four cats nodded, and then the two white angel buddies disappeared behind the curtains.

After a short while, we heard the sound of thousands of cats arriving at the Heavenly Cat Auditorium. There was a lot of kitty chatter taking place. Clearly, no one had any idea of the purpose for this meeting.

The meeting began with a loud cat meow followed by a sudden hush in the audience. Willie nudged my paw as the pure-white angel buddies took their places behind the podium at the corner of the stage.

"Good morning to all angel cats here in Cat Heaven," one of them announced. "We have gathered today to tell you about an incredible Earthly wish that was completed by two angel cats." The audience was silent.

"This story is going to change what we do in Cat Heaven, and possibly give many of you the chance to follow this dream," announced the other pure-white angel buddy. "Rather than wasting any more time, I will turn the meeting over to Chloe and Oscar."

There was a buzz in the audience as Chloe and Oscar crossed the stage. Chloe began telling our story. She started with me searching for the perfect Earthly wish to complete, something that I didn't get a chance to do when I was on Earth.

"Minka wanted to travel back to Earth to protect her friends from harm and danger. I told her that wouldn't be possible, that such a wish had never been requested or granted to an angel cat before."

Then Oscar chimed in, talking about how Willie had asked to complete the same wish without knowing what lay ahead of him. The cat audience chuckled, knowing what a headstrong cat Willie could be.

Chloe and Oscar went on to explain how the Angel Leaders decided to grant our wish, and told of the five sacred rules, the building of our wings, the training, the test flights, and finally the heroic events on Earth. There was complete silence among the angel cats in the audience.

Chloe ended by saying, "I want you all to meet our two heroes."

A set of curtains opened. Willie and I heard wild applause as soon as the audience saw us sitting in the royal chairs. A second set of curtains revealed our encased wings. The cat audience gasped and meowed in excitement.

Oscar held up a paw for silence. "Now, let's watch a few of Minka and Willie's heroic episodes on Earth." The final set of curtains opened, and beautiful music played as our images appeared on the screen. We watched as our wings were built and then magically appeared on our backs, our test flights, and the two of us flying off into the horizon. There were scenes from each of the four cat visits

up to the final moment when each wish was completed for our cat friends.

We heard boisterous meows from the audience, as well as applause, oohs and ahs, and even tears and whimpers. The angel cats seemed mesmerized, excited, and amazed as they watched the story of our Earthly wish. When the video ended, the audience jumped on top of their seats, and cheers rocked the auditorium.

"Hush, hush," exclaimed Oscar. "We have an important announcement to make!"

The audience hushed and once again took their seats as Oscar and Chloe explained the new program called Friend Watch. "This program is intended to extend the goodwill we teach our angel cats in Cat Heaven. Our hope is that all cats on Earth will have angels watching over them," remarked Chloe. "The guidelines to qualify for this program are very strict."

The announcement was greeted by a lot of buzz in the auditorium. Angel cats began to talk to one another and search for their angel buddies.

"Please—there is an order to all this excitement," exclaimed Chloe. "At the end of this meeting you will be able to locate your angel buddy at the back of the auditorium to sign up for the screening of Friend Watch."

Oscar called once again for silence. It was time to announce the positions we had chosen in Cat Heaven. The audience meowed in excitement.

"Willie has decided to become an angel buddy," Oscar announced proudly. I looked over at Willie and then nibbled his paw. Willie nudged my head. Oscar went on. "Willie and I will be in charge of your social entertainment. Every Friday we will be performing at the auditorium for an Angel Cat Dance Night. This way we can decompress from our hectic week and socialize with other angel cats."

I applauded with the others. Willie's dream of performing in a rock band had come true!

It was Chloe's turn to announce my choice. "Minka is going to fill a vacancy at the Angel Castle." Willie gasped. There was complete silence in the auditorium. "She will become the eighth Angel Leader," Chloe said quietly. "I knew that Minka was a very special angel cat when I first met her. I had no idea of the journey I would complete with her, but I knew that her powers and insights were extraordinary."

Willie clutched my paw.

"Minka will be in charge of making sure there are enough angel cats to cover all the needs down on Earth. She has the passion, patience, and perseverance to make this new program succeed."

I heard Willie whisper, "The Angel Leaders knew it was you from the very start. They were just testing you to see if you had what it takes to join them. You will be a great Angel Leader. I love you, Minka."

He nudged my forehead, and I purred. "I love you too, Willie."

"Let's applaud our heroes," Chloe said. The cat audience stood on top of their seats and loudly cheered and applauded. "The meeting is adjourned. Please locate your angel buddy in the back of the auditorium."

All the cats ran up to the stage and swarmed around Willie and me. A long line formed as each cat congratulated us on our heroic events on Earth as well as our new positions in Cat Heaven. Every cat wanted to touch us, as though some kind of magic would rub off on them.

As soon as they jumped off the stage, most of the cats rushed to the back of the auditorium to meet with their angel buddies and sign up for the new program.

Willie and I stayed onstage until the last angel cat had congratulated us and left the Heavenly Cat Auditorium. The four of us stood next to each other in silence.

Oscar was the first to speak. "Whew, what an event. Minka, I am so very proud of you. Don't get too caught up in all that leadership stuff and forget to visit us!"

"I will be seeing you often," I told him. "Willie, let's make a playdate each week. You can come and visit me at the Angel Castle."

Willie looked pleased. "Very cool. I can play you my latest tunes."

"I would like that very much," I purred.

Oscar turned to Willie. "Let's get started on teaching you to become an angel buddy!" Instantly, beautiful feathered wings outlined in gold appeared on Willie's back. They made a soft lulling sound.

"Willie," I exclaimed, "you look amazing."

Willie leaned over and hugged me very close. "Thank you, Minka, for helping me go from my short life on Earth to this place in Cat Heaven, and for taking care of me. We will see each other very soon."

"Soon it will be," I whispered softly.

With a few twirls and swirls, Oscar and Willie flew out of the auditorium in the direction of the angel cat clouds.

That left Chloe and I facing each other. "The Angel Leaders are waiting for you, Minka," she said. At once, large gold wings appeared on my back and a gold halo hovered over my head. I turned to look at my wings. At the slightest movement, they released an abundance of golden sparkles that covered my entire body and then dispersed into the air.

"You have been an amazing friend," Chloe said. "I will miss seeing you, but I am proud to have had the privilege of serving you. You are a magical cat and deserve to take your place in the Angel Castle."

I leaned over and nudged Chloe's head. Chloe purred.

"Now go. You know the way," she meowed.

I looked at Chloe. I, too, felt very tearful. "Thank you, my dear friend, for helping me find the path I must follow."

"You always knew the path. A soft lullaby was singing in your heart." Chloe bowed her head. I looked at Chloe one last time. Instantly, I was flying in the air, out of the Heavenly Cat Auditorium and north in the direction of the Angel Castle.

I flew above angel clouds that went on for miles and miles. All the angel clouds were surrounded by a magical fog. I flew past the part of Cat Heaven that housed the angel cats, and forward into the shimmering light. I could feel the powerful force of Cat Heaven in the air. In the far distance, the glittering Angel Castle appeared on top of a huge magical cloud. The vibrant colors of the castle flickered throughout the air.

I pointed my head up and, with as much speed as I could, raised myself higher into the air. Then I curled my body tightly and did a somersault. My wings released an abundance of golden sparkles. I squealed with sheer joy.

I quickly pointed my left ear to make a left turn and then my right ear to make a sharp right turn. I lifted my head to get more speed before flicking my tail to make two circles in the shape of a figure eight. My wings released more golden sparkles that shot into the air. I pointed my head in the direction of the Angel Castle and started my descent.

Before I reached the gates of the Angel Castle, I peered back down at Earth. I thought about all the cats on Earth, especially Muris, Casper, Sofia, and Zarah.

"Dear friends, we will be watching over you from Cat Heaven," I called out.

I curled my body into a tight ball and did two somersaults in a row. When I looked down at Earth, I felt a peaceful feeling rush through my soul. As I purred, I saw my wings release a sparkling cloud of golden stars that floated into the air and down to Earth.

Now I knew what they were—good wishes and blessings for all the cats I cared about. Good friends live forever in our hearts.

The End

About the Author

Valda V. Upenieks received her PhD from the University of Washington and has worked in various nurse leadership and consulting roles throughout the country. She has two daughters, Laura and Lasma, and they live in the greater Seattle area with their two dogs, Percy and Pedro, and two cats.

~~~~~~

Review Requested:
If you loved this book, would you please provide a review at Amazon.com?

Thank You

Printed in the USA
CPSIA information can be obtained
at www.ICGtesting.com
LVHW071634020224
770787LV00003B/359